WHILE GODS ARE FALLING

ALSO BY EARL LOVELACE

WHILE GODS ARE FALLING

EARL LOVELACE

INTRODUCTION BY J. DILLON BROWN

PEEPAL TREE

First published in Great Britain in 1965
by Collins
This new edition published in 2011
Peepal Tree Press Ltd
17 King's Avenue
Leeds LS6 1QS
England

ISBN13: 9781845231484

Supported by
ARTS COUNCIL
ENGLAND

INTRODUCTION

J. DILLON BROWN

For readers and scholars of Caribbean literature, the most appropriate response to the republication of Earl Lovelace's *While Gods Are Falling* might simply be gratitude. Gratitude, certainly, for the plain fact that Lovelace's debut novel will again be available to read and study without having to chase down a copy in the library or, more desperately, scour the tricky bookselling back-channels for a rare (and expensive) out-of-print edition: the book is far too important to be relegated to the publishing equivalent of what Lovelace himself might term second-classness. But gratitude, also, because such a response – a simple, but profoundly meaningful affirmation, simultaneously recognizing and embodying an act of communal enrichment – is not only the reaction that Lovelace's work has consistently drawn from its readers, but an example of the values it has sought to uphold. From the 1965 publication of *While Gods Are Falling*, across four more novels and one collection each of short stories, plays, and essays, to his just-released novel of 2011, *Is Just a Movie*, Lovelace's writing has explicitly aimed to foster a critical, but ultimately affirmative sense of shared human purpose. As Lovelace has himself averred, an author is 'someone whose power and duty is simply, with compassion and firmness, to call us to account as humans, and to tenaciously insist that we honour the highest ideal of what it is to be human' (*Growing in the Dark*, p. 173). Although such exhortations toward moral uplift might initially seem naïve, the emphasis on firmness and tenacity must also be acknowledged. In Lovelace's work, the steady insistence that 'we need to learn to cherish each other' (*Growing*, p. 54) is never reducible to the simple or the sentimental: his call to solidarity is always complicated by an acute awareness of both the historically grounded structural forces working against social cohesion in the Caribbean, as well as the majority of people's wilful reluctance to counteract these forces in their everyday lives. Although sometimes disregarded by critics as apprentice work, *While Gods Are Falling* richly displays such critical and aesthetic complexity, a complexity that lies at the heart of Earl Lovelace's expressive vision of the possibilities for an ethical, humane Caribbean community. In this first novel, Lovelace expresses his political vision more directly than he does in any of his subsequent fiction. This is perhaps not so much a sign that Lovelace's fiction grows more subtle (though it does), but that having expressed his position, he feels no need to reiterate it. He may also have felt that by the time he published his later work, the turbulent and disappointing political realities of the post-independence republic made these points for him. *While Gods Are Falling* was written at a moment when at least some of his fellow countrymen and women still dwelt within the euphoric hopes of independence. As this introduction outlines, Lovelace's vision of the shortcomings of his nation's approach to the project of independence is both insightful and prophetic, and thus remains relevant to an understanding of the travails of Caribbean nation-states today. In this light, we should indeed be grateful for the renewed chance offered by this edition to witness Lovelace's resolutely clear-eyed, insistently kindhearted vision in its earliest iteration.

One indication of the complexity with which Lovelace grapples as a writer can be found in the historical context out of which *While Gods Are Falling* was published. Lovelace, at the time an agricultural ministry worker living in rural Tobago, submitted the manuscript of the novel – previously rejected by several foreign publishers – for the British Petroleum Independence Literary Award, a prize meant to honour the first anniversary of the date of Trinidad and Tobago's formal political independence on August 31, 1962. The selection of his manuscript as the winner of the competition in 1964 brought with it a cash prize and considerable recognition, while officially inaugurating Lovelace's authorial career in the form of publication with the London publisher, Collins, in 1965. The irony of this situation, whereby an author resolutely committed to radical decolonisation gets his professional start via the imprimatur of an iconic corporate representative of British imperial (and neo-colonial) power, is difficult to overlook (perhaps acquiring further contemporary resonance in the aftermath of the horrific 2010 oil spill resulting from the accident involving BP's Deepwater Horizon well in the Gulf of Mexico). The irreconcilable tensions that it suggests – between British and Caribbean, metropolitan and regional, modern and traditional, wealthy and impoverished, urban and rural – of course, animate Lovelace's work with particular poignancy, not least in this, his first novel. In such a light, Lovelace's work falls squarely into the lineage of the 'Windrush' generation of writers such as George Lamming, Edgar Mittelholzer, Andrew Salkey, and Sam Selvon, who were paradoxically forced to rely in part on the institutional support of metropolitan Britain (especially the BBC and London's commercial publishing houses) in order to convey their anti-colonial, nationalist literary messages. Selvon's 1970 novel, *The Plains of Caroni*, sponsored by the sugar company Caroni, Ltd. as a celebration of Trinidad and Tobago's Agricultural Year, might be seen as a sibling text to *While Gods Are Falling*. Although Lovelace's novel was already written before its submission for the BP award, whereas Selvon's was written as a consequence of Caroni Ltd. funding, both novels raise similar issues about the messy matrix of art, commerce, and state-sponsorship in which Caribbean literature (like all literature) takes form, and the fitful and irregular structures of institutional support generally available to writers in the region. Unlike his 'Windrush' predecessors, however, Lovelace's writing career has taken place wholly *after* independence had been gained for his home island, and also almost wholly *within* his island. Apart from a period of study at Howard and Johns Hopkins universities, and a residency at the Writers Program at the University of Iowa, Lovelace has lived continuously in Trinidad. Firmly rooted in post-independence island life, Lovelace makes no recourse to easy, emotive calls for liberation from colonial oppression, because, at least in official terms, Trinidad and Tobago is free to act as it will. It is within these cultural and historical currents that *While Gods Are Falling* becomes particularly interesting and important with regard to the Anglophone Caribbean literary tradition: it is a novel confronting many of the same themes of inequality and oppression as its predecessors, but at a moment in which the understanding of those themes is increasingly being shifted into the frame of actually existing national independence. As this introduction will suggest, Lovelace's particular rootedness in place and time indelibly shapes his vision.

Independence – as it relates to the demands of history, as well as to the responsibilities of community – is the pivotal concern of *While Gods Are Falling*. The novel's protagonist, Walter Castle, is introduced to the reader as an angry, disheartened man, fed up with his lot in life and chafing under an inarticulate sense of oppression. In his first, strained conversation with his wife, Stephanie, Walter employs the imagery of impotent captivity to describe his state, saying, 'Look, a man has to begin somewhere, some time. You can't just keep crawlin' around trying, slaving, just to stay alive so you can pay the rent and quiet the worms inside you' (p. 28; all page references to this edition). Unwilling to submit any longer to the perceived indignity of his working life, Walter defines his very humanity in terms of independence, arguing that 'if a man don't have something like steel inside him that they can't touch and they can't bend, then he's a robot, something to be switched on and switched off' (p. 29). The solution Walter proposes to his dilemma – connected in the early pages of the novel with his perception of the rot at the core of the city of Port of Spain itself – is simply to leave, move to the country, and live off the land. Unmoved by Stephanie's pragmatic concerns for the family (including their small daughter and the unborn child she is carrying), Walter can only articulate independence as a reflexive, largely inchoate desire to escape. As he angrily informs Stephanie: 'All I'm thinking is a way to get out. Get away from the job, the people and this city. That's all. Get away' (p. 30). The rest of the novel, unfolding slowly over the events of the next few days, represents Walter's – and Lovelace's – anguished meditations on the nature of independence and the moral validity of, as Stephanie describes it, simply 'running away' (p. 30).

Walter's initial impulse to flee bears a complicated relation to the past. On the one hand, Walter is seeking to escape his own past – he bristles against the helplessness and indignity of poverty that he experienced as a child. As the novel reveals in the first of many flashbacks, the agricultural accident his father suffers when Walter is a small boy condemns the entire family to a tense, precarious form of subsistence. Pap's sense of helplessness, futility, and rage cast a pall over the household as it struggles to survive, caught in an endless cycle of poverty: 'there was a kind of silence about the house like a net, and a kind of anxiety in the air, as if everyone was waiting for something to happen' (p. 38). What happens, of course, are the diverse, occasionally happy trials of everyday life, but the burden of supporting the family without Pap's labour, accompanied by the insistent threat of dispossession and hunger, weigh heavily on Walter and his family, ultimately leading to misunderstanding and far-reaching estrangement. On the other hand, Walter's plan for escape actually involves the return, in a sense, to his past, related both to his early rural childhood and the agrarian retreat of his young manhood in the village of Nuggle. Lovelace's extended depiction of Walter's dreamlike vision of pastoral bliss suggests how sentimental and oversimplified his protagonist's relation to the past actually is:

> In his mind he sees the countryside so quiet. The earth is wet, and the grass is green and glistens with dew and sunlight. The corn is tall and the ears are long, and blonde hair hangs out from the tassels. Birds are singing in a mango tree, the mist is disappearing, the chickens rush for feed and scatter when the dog jumps. The cow is being milked and the potatoes are being hoed and there is a big pumpkin under the avocado tree. Smoke comes from a wood fire and rises to the blue sky. The children bathe in the river and lie down on the bank and laugh, or look at the silver

water running over the smooth stones on the riverbed and wait
for the coscorob to glide out from beneath the stone. The wind
rushes, trees lean and shake; the doves coo and walk on the
ground, in pairs. (p. 134)

The passage calls particular attention to the vision's sources in
Walter's past experience, with the quiet plenty of nature and
the laughing children recalling his initial experience of Nuggle,
while the pairs of doves explicitly evoke the two doves Walter
catches in the forest as a young boy just before moving to
Jerico. Moreover, there is a noticeable absence of adult humans – all the labour is rendered in the passive voice, as if
happening by magic – and the subtle emphasis at the beginning
on how this is all 'in his mind' likewise suggests the wishful,
unreal nature of Walter's hasty dreams of rural salvation. In
this pattern there is an interesting contrast with Selvon's novel,
Turn Again Tiger, written in 1958. Here Tiger is both in flight
from the rural past, and bitterly opposed to re-entering
renewed servitude to agricultural labour and its indignities.
Tiger, though, tricked into a return, discovers a community he
has been unable to imagine. Perhaps only a writer who had left
Trinidad a decade earlier could envisage such a return.

Of course, as in nearly all of Lovelace's novels, the countryside quickly reveals the lie of such romanticization. Just like
The Schoolmaster's Kumaca, *The Wine of Astonishment*'s Bonasse,
or *Salt*'s Cascadu and Cunaripo, the village of Nuggle cannot be
reduced to a bucolic rural stereotype. Indeed, as Walter grows
to realize in remembering his time at Nuggle, it was just as full
of vice and petty jealousies and self-interest as Port of Spain
itself, and, just as importantly, the village cannot escape the
reach of technical and political modernization urged on by the
nascent governing party (here named, inauspiciously, the Party
of National Importance, though clearly meant to evoke Eric
Williams's People's National Movement). This is certainly not
to suggest that the countryside is dismissed as corrupted in the
novel, only that it cannot, for Lovelace, serve as an unproblematic
space of timeless, unsullied redemption. The present is present,
as it were, in both locations, and Walter must confront it

wherever he wishes to stake a claim to life. This attention to the present is characteristic of all of Lovelace's novels: whether it is in the arena of Bolo's stickfighting in *The Wine of Astonishment*, Aldrick's playing mas in *The Dragon Can't Dance*, or Adolphe Carabon's halfhearted continuation of plantation agriculture in *Salt*, Lovelace's novels consistently insist on the need for thoughtful adaptation in the face of historical change. If the physical immobility of Walter in the first half of *While Gods Are Falling* symbolically echoes that of his father after the tractor accident, Walter's impulse to run away as the novel begins is likewise shown to be a recurrence of his previous behaviour: he has, it emerges, largely spent his life impatiently running away. Over the course of *While Gods Are Falling*, Lovelace carefully conveys how Walter's initial desire for a superficially fresh start is emphatically not a break with the past, but rather an unproductive reconfirmation of its recalcitrant reach. In this we may perhaps see the shaping consciousness of a writer who, unlike Selvon, has never gone away.

If the novel makes plain that Walter's facile desires to remain free from history would be self-defeating, it also underscores the troubling implications of Walter's vision of independence for any workable concept of community. And here it is worth noting that whilst *While Gods Are Falling* has a good deal to say (sometimes implicitly) about what Lovelace sees as the grievous flaws of the independence project as led by the island's political leaders – the top-downness that would become authoritarian and the failure to involve the people other than as ethnic vote-banks – it is with the failure of ordinary people to seize the responsibility for the future that the novel is most concerned. Walter's wife and family, of course, represent the book's most telling critique of its protagonist's conception of independence as faulty. Stephanie's immediate reaction to Walter's announcement that he wants to quit his job and move away is to look down at her belly, silently suggesting that he consider the effect such a decision has on others. She emphasizes her sympathy with Walter's predicament, indicating a level of pointedly individualized concern: 'for *your* sake I would like to agree because I feel it means a lot to *you*' (p. 32, emphasis added). However, she proceeds to suggest that her own status with regard to others – 'one baby in my hand and one in my belly' (p. 32) – makes acceding to Walter's individual desires an untenable option: she is too closely, intimately, and even physically, linked to others to simply escape. Later in the novel, Stephanie makes the point in a slightly different way, explaining to Walter that he, too, is irrevocably bound up in the world: 'you see, you can't take from the world and not pay. You cannot take one part and reject the other' (p. 133). In response, Walter asks what he has taken from the world, to which Stephanie replies, 'you have a wife. You have a child and you expect another…' (p. 133). Couching her claim in a language of debt and obligation that prefigures *Salt*'s interest in both the material and the spiritual aspects of reparation, Stephanie again insists to Walter that he cannot but think of himself in relation to others. This discussion sparks the first inklings of Walter's epiphany in the novel, as Lovelace traces his protagonist's train of thought shortly after this scene: 'So, this world is mine, he thinks. And this land is mine and the people here are my people, and the things that are done in this city – I am also responsible for them. I am one with the land and I am one with the people' (p. 135). This realization – an acceptance of responsibility and belonging – contrasts markedly with Walter's previous attitude of rejection and flight, and it is the central moment in the plot of *While Gods Are Falling* (and indeed occurs, in a literal sense, in the centre of the novel). From this point on, the novel traces the gradual process whereby Walter learns to accept that independence can never truly be absolute, that he will only be able to make sense of himself individually by seeing himself as a part of something communal.

In this way, Walter appears as a literary ancestor to the protagonist of Caryl Phillips's *A State of Independence* (1986), Bertram Francis, who is similarly lost and angry – and similarly prone to drinking, listlessness, and a type of selfishly juvenile rebellion. Both characters ultimately realize that independence *from* something, in being a strictly negative and reactive disposition, is an unproductive notion. In both Phillips's novel and *While Gods Are Falling*, it is only via a recognition of interdependence and relation that one can finally be independent enough to do something meaningful. Both Lovelace and Phillips figure these relations most immediately at the level of family. In addition to Stephanie, Walter's brother Andrew, though hardly a perfect spokesperson for consensual community building, remonstrates with Walter about his lack of sensitivity to family ties, angrily saying, 'Don't know what get in your head to take up and leave home an' run away thinking you's a man, to go on your own like an ownerless dog' (p. 71). Andrew's wrath, though rash and unsubtle, does have some justification, considering the sacrifices he himself has made to pay for Walter's education, only to have the latter abandon the family and cut off nearly all communication. Later in the novel, Andrew softens his tone, apologising to Walter for being so unbendingly strict and acknowledging the lessons he has learned about clinging to his own ideas. He confesses to Walter that it took a long time for him to recognise that he alone 'didn't make the world for one thing. And for another that alone, a man don't feel good. People need people' (p. 164). Andrew's language – with contrasting values ascribed to dogs and people – reinforces the novel's sense that respectful interrelation is at the very core of what it means to be human (and, relatedly, of course, humane). At this moment of rapprochement between the brothers, Andrew suggests that some effort needs to be made to rebuild the family, because 'when a man doesn't belong, when he has to fight alone, achievements don't mean a thing' (p. 164). By the end of the novel Walter, in conversation with Andrew, fully adopts his brother's outlook, accepting the blame for failing to help raise their younger brother Chris and saying, 'We didn't give him a thing. We just lived by ourselves, for ourselves' (p. 221). Paradoxically perhaps, in *While Gods Are Falling*, the mutual reciprocity of family life functions as the necessary foundation for articulating a meaningful selfhood.

For Lovelace, of course, the ethical demands of community do not stop at the level of family. As *While Gods Are Falling* makes clear, a wider commitment is required: social bonds well beyond the family have been sundered and are in need of

13

reparation. It is certainly possible to see in what Andrew learns about true authority, as opposed to authoritarianism, Lovelace's warnings on the direction of the political leadership in Trinidad under Williams, a leadership that was increasingly displaying signs of an intemperate deafness to other opinions, and a 'hero's' disposition towards a supposedly adulatory 'crowd'. Ominously, the twin spectres of poverty and crime haunt the novel, serving as an externalized manifestation of Walter's own uncertainty and anger. Indeed, the novel introduces the sense of threat permeating Port of Spain even before it introduces its protagonist, and takes its very title from this widespread malaise. After beginning with a brief description of the grand and beautiful aspects of the city, the narrative turns its attention abruptly to the less fortunate areas of Port of Spain, describing how,

> it is not only poverty. It is disorder; it is crime; it is a kind of fear, and a way of thinking; it is as if there is a special, narrow meaning to life, as if life has no significance beyond the primary struggles for a bed to sleep in, something to quiet the intestines, and moments of sexual gratification: indeed, it is as if all Gods have fallen and there is nothing to look up to, no shrine to worship at, and man is left only bare flesh and naked passions. (p. 22)

The stark, elemental imagery used to portray the city here inaugurates the novel's view that something essentially human is lacking in the social world it describes: a broader, more ennobling understanding of life's purpose is deemed necessary. Before introducing Walter for the first time, the novel bluntly summarizes this assessment, repeating its critiques of the population's widespread indifference to others, but also asserting that 'there is something else here, something dark, poisonous and stinking, something like a sore in this city' (p. 23). Here, it is possible to see Lovelace putting himself in a Caribbean tradition of moral prophecy best characterised by Roger Mais's *The Hills Were Joyful Together* (1953). Such a despairing view of Port of Spain – resonant, sadly, to contemporary ears – appears to find its main object of critique in urban youth culture, dominated by what Walter and his neighbour Mr. Cross derisively describe as 'hooligans' (p. 22). Certainly, the novel seems unabashed in acknowledging the existence of callous violence committed by young men ruthlessly disrespectful of social mores, describing how 'young men, angry and evil, arm themselves with knives, iron bolts, cutlasses and revolvers, and chop and smash and shoot and riot, and sometimes somebody is killed' (p. 23). It is an urban darkness touched on in the episodes of violence in the novels of A.H. Mendes (*Black Fauns*, 1935) and C.L.R. James (*Minty Alley*, 1936) and in some of the early stories of Sam Selvon such as 'Steelband', 'Carnival Last Lap' and 'Murder Will Out' (*Trinidad Guardian*, 25 May, 1947, 8 Feb., 1948 and 24 April 1948, respectively). However, the introduction of Walter immediately after evoking the city's malady suggests, rather, that it is with Walter himself, and others like him, that the fault may lie. Indeed, by the book's end this hypothesis seems plainly confirmed. The major change in the novel does not take place on a grandiose social scale. It is instead a change in Walter himself. As he finally returns to his office on Tuesday, after his momentous agreement to help his neighbour's son and organize the community to help itself, Walter realizes that the change starts from within, and often only on a small, personal scale: 'There are the usual faces, the usual hellos and grins. There is nothing here to indicate any change. Nothing in the office has changed. It is he that changed. It is he that is new, if anything is new' (p. 249). What is most strikingly new about Walter, moreover, is his attitude toward his own downtrodden, poverty-stricken neighbourhood, especially its young men. At the start of the novel Walter finds himself repelled by his young male neighbours' behaviour: 'They curse drivers for going by too slowly, and show a ruthless disrespect for age and sex' (p. 24). By the book's end, Walter argues, against Stephanie's fearful protestations, that they must be involved in helping precisely the neighbours from whom they have been separating themselves, saying, 'these people, Stephanie, are the people around us. They are the people we know and have to know' (p. 217). Indeed, Walter's political project focuses on helping

15

the neighbourhood's young 'hooligans', whom he and many others have simply dismissed and rejected over the course of the novel. After visiting one of these boys in prison – Ruben, his downstairs neighbour – Walter is awakened by a sense of communal responsibility. In describing his visit to Mr. Cross, Walter says, 'I had no idea that I would either be in this, or want to be in this, but I went to see one of the boys in prison, and I thought that I was in some way responsible for what happened, not to that boy alone, but to all the boys in this area, because I have never done anything to assist them' (p. 226). For Walter, such action is not to be seen as simply charity or kindheartedness, but as a responsibility. More importantly, it is a form of self-actualization, a conscious action catalyzing the creation of an autonomous community. As Walter emphasizes, in helping the boys 'the people will be helping themselves' (p. 228), which would seem to be the novel's primary moral imperative. In *While Gods Are Falling*, social problems cannot be alone attributed to government, 'hooligans', the former colonial masters, or others of any kind – at a fundamental level, the novel suggests, everyone must take some responsibility, and following that, some action.

This appeal to involvement is, in literary terms, most apparent in the novel's use of the unusual second-person mode of address at its beginning and end. The effect of this technique – perhaps familiar to contemporary readers from Jamaica Kincaid's assertive use of it to accost white Anglo-American readers in *A Small Place* (1988) – is that of a direct address, rhetorically instantiating the reader as an interlocutor and participant. Specifically hailed by the text, the reader is not allowed the comfort of mere observation but is, in some sense, held answerable for what is witnessed. For Lovelace's novel, the purpose of this address seems clear: if you are reading this book, you too must confront the problems it portrays. Such an address formally reiterates the message of communal responsibility, putting the onus not on the young, poor, and hope-deprived underclass, but on people like Walter – the literate, white-collar, professional class, or, plainly, the people most likely to be reading the novel in the first place. And here, though the novel was published in London, Lovelace may have had a greater than average justification (because of the prize and his presence there) for feeling that his primary readership ought to be Trinidadian. It is no accident that Walter himself is first described as a 'brown-skinned little man' (p. 23): such an epithet indicates his relative placement within the subtly graded racial hierarchy of Trinidad and Tobago, and implicitly suggests that he is a small man, not only physically but also in the social scale of power. However, as the novel makes clear, though Walter is a minor bureaucrat with little power at the national level, he and Stephanie, along with Mr. Cross, display all the signs of relative privilege vis a vis their immediate surroundings. It is this group – what would be called the lower middle-class in the United States – that seems to be addressed most directly by the novel and urged to act. Lovelace calls upon these people to lead by upright, righteous example, since the 'bigger' people – the government ministers and representatives, the clerisy, and the wealthy business community – have failed to do so. As Lovelace's narrator angrily observes, shadowing Walter's disconsolate thoughts after his failed attempt to recruit Mr. Cross to his cause:

> in this city, in this island, the gods are falling and there is nothing for the young people to look up to – nothing for anyone to look up to. The leading citizens are wrapped in their self-centredness, and life is the extension of the individual's personality – a sort of emotional masturbation; and love is something you can crease and slip in your wallet; and pride is something that on Sunday morning you wash with a garden hose and shine, having polished. (p. 229)

In its diagnosis of social ills, this passage emphasizes the coarsening and degradation emanating from the very top of the social ladder – the leaders have abandoned responsibility for their fellow citizens, and their superficial, selfish values have triumphed. Walter's small but valiant resistance to these trends at the end of the novel is thus seen to be the potential beginnings of a possible answer to this problem. The novel's second-person narration leaves little doubt that the reader, too, is being beckoned to follow in these nascent acts of solidarity and community building.

To contemporary ears, the borders of this imagined solidarity are restricted. Certainly, women are not given particularly prominent roles in the novel's final prescriptions. The chiasmus that characterizes Walter and Stephanie's relationship over the course of the novel is one indication of this unevenness. In the beginning, Walter is the irrational and impatient one, while Stephanie gently and wisely urges him to reconsider. By the end, it is Walter who insists on and embodies the novel's communal values, while Stephanie hysterically shrinks from contact with 'the people' and is reduced to absolute silence at the climactic political meeting. The one female member of the neighbourhood's informal leadership committee is asked to join because, in Walter's words, 'though she's a woman, she has good ideas about this kinda thing' (p. 224). Like many of Lovelace's novels, *While Gods Are Falling* portrays a strong sense of individual self via extremely masculine imagery, exemplified in this case by Walter's persistent association of his 'balls' with his social autonomy. Perhaps more alarming is the seemingly casual dismissal of the person murdered by the 'tesses' in the novel. These alleged assailants, guilty or otherwise, are the express object of Walter's politicised concern, in stark contrast to the 'homo' who is killed. Quickly, almost dismissively forgotten, this unnamed victim is perhaps the only character to escape humanising, sympathetic treatment in the novel, subject instead to the callous logic of Andrew's summary of the event: 'You know how it is with these homos. They try to encourage these boys. Well, he got a good beating' (pp. 220). Andrew's rather alarming understatement, and his implicit acceptance of the justice of the boys' actions, reveals traces of the violent homophobia that still bedevils the Caribbean today. These small but significant details suggest some troubling limitations to the novel's notions of national belonging.

However, it is certainly the nation – specifically Trinidad and Tobago – with which Lovelace is concerned. More than many other Anglophone Caribbean authors, Lovelace has been associated with a dedication to the local and the national. Unlike the created composite islands of writers such as Lamming and V.S. Naipaul, the setting in each of Lovelace's novels is concretely his home country, with roughly equal attention, overall, given to both its urban and the rural spaces. For Lovelace, it is, in fact, only via an active linking of these two spaces that any meaningful sense of national belonging can be summoned. If *While Gods Are Falling* locates the space of meaningful change for Walter in the capital city of Port of Spain, its impulse toward human interconnection is shared by all of Lovelace's work. This interconnection is the necessary substance of nationhood, which Lovelace envisions as a perennial process, 'not something to be achieved, but something to strive for constantly' (*Growing,* p. 159). As *While Gods Are Falling* insists, this process can only begin at the level of the local and the everyday. At the end of the novel, as he strolls confidently to the neighbourhood meeting he has organised, Walter and Stephanie see a group of young men up ahead lurking, somewhat threateningly, in their path, and clearly having no intention of attending the meeting. Against Stephanie's fearful inclination to cross to the other side of the street, Walter insists they continue on their path. The polite respect Walter offers to these boys – not fearing them, addressing them as equals – is ultimately reciprocated, and he reminds them about the meeting. The novel closes with the small triumph of this interaction, in which the young men, like Walter, suddenly inhabit a new dignity and purpose: 'The set of their shoulders and the swing of their hands and the way they hold their heads. Those boys are coming to the meeting' (p. 255). It is out of this mutual respect, however tentative and uncertain, that Lovelace sees post-independence national community being built. In Lovelace's thinking, if we are to accomplish anything worthwhile, 'we have to face each other, with frailty and courage and grace' (*Growing,* p. 200). *While Gods Are Falling* asks us to do precisely this.

J. Dillon Brown
Washington University in St. Louis

WORKS CITED

Lovelace, Earl. *While Gods Are Falling*. London: Collins, 1965.
____. *Growing in the Dark (Selected Essays)*. Funso Aiyejina, ed.
San Juan: Lexington, Trinidad, Ltd., 2003

1

You stand there on the top-floor landing of the three-storeyed tenement building on Webber Street, look out at the city of Port of Spain.

Above the tangle of black electric wires, tops of taller buildings rise under the heavily clouded sky. There is the Anglican Cathedral, and there is one Roman Catholic Cathedral, and over there another; and down there is the Treasury building near the harbour where small craft stir and larger ships lie at anchor; and across there is the Salvatori building, towering above other structures. That to your right is the General Hospital; and that is the Queen's Park Hotel, and across from it the Queen's Park Savannah spread like a green carpet made greener by the presence of the whitewashed rails of the horse-race track; and behind it is St Clair with green-roofed, white Victorian houses in yards with green shade-trees, mown lawns, well-trimmed hedges and pedigree dogs sprawled before kennels, with heads upon outstretched front paws, grudgingly grumbling at flies that would break the peace of their laziness. Away to the right is the Belmont hillside, and that building, elegant like a tall, well-dressed young man, handsome in his clothes, is the modern Trinidad Hilton Hotel. (They say there is a panoramic view of the city from every room.) You will see the city better from there. And though on this morning the skies are cluttered with thick black clouds, the green mountains skirting the scene are caught up in mist and wetness clings to every roof and is on every pavement, you can feel tall, for this is your city.

But turn your head. Look at the Laventille hillside where damp small houses balance with a sort of perpetual excitement, appearing to draw from strong winds both respect and compassion.

Look, and feel anger building within you, bulging your neck veins, bristling your neck hairs, feel the blood of anger thumping in your ears – this is your city too. On those hills there, it is not only poverty. It is disorder; it is crime; it is a kind of fear, and a way of thinking; it is as if there is a special, narrow meaning to life, as if life has no significance beyond the primary struggles for a bed to sleep in, something to quiet the intestines, and moments of sexual gratification: indeed, it is as if all Gods have fallen and there is nothing to look up to, no shrine to worship at, and man is left only bare flesh and naked passions.

And that is not all. This disorder and poverty and crime, this kind of fear and this way of thinking – particularly this way of thinking – all reach down like rivers from the hills, on all sides, to Quarry Street and to Bishop's Place and Merry Street and beyond to Nelson and George Streets. Yes, and this way of thinking is true of young and old, and the middle-aged are not exempt from it. And there is no decrease in disorder and crime, and no end to fear, even though more policemen with more revolvers are patrolling the areas, even though magistrates are dealing harshly with persons guilty of crimes of sex and violence; though priests are saying more masses, and, in Woodford Square and on pavements wayside preachers sweat and holler 'Set your house in order!' The world will end tomorrow or next Wednesday week; and in the daily papers, various self-appointed psychologists are blaming government, parents, teachers, priests, and the leniency of magistrates; and some talk detachedly of the influences of London and the United States, unemployment, and the fall of morality in the younger generation.

And alongside this, on the other side of the city – around St Clair, at Elleslie Park, Petit Valley and so on – people are buying more motor cars, TV sets, washing machines, and, sipping whisky or gin, in forced English and low tones mumble of the criminal situation in the island. And their radios keep saying: 'Port of Spain is a beautiful city. Port of Spain is the richest city in the Caribbean. Trinidad is the birthplace of the steel-band, and the authentic land of the calypso. Come to our shores, watch our girls do the limbo.' And so on, and so on.

What is wrong with this city? What is the mystery here? At

nights, on the Laventille hillside, down Quarry Street, Bishop's Place, and even on Webber, Nelson and George Streets, young men rich with rhythm send music slanting like frightened grasshoppers off steel drums. At night, too, from these very areas, young men, angry and evil, arm themselves with knives, iron bolts, cutlasses and revolvers, and chop and smash and shoot and riot, and sometimes somebody is killed. How is this?

There is something wrong in this city. There is something that underlies the problems of disorder and crime, and there is something responsible for the fear and for the way of thinking. And they will tell you that your city is rich, beautiful, and that the steel-band is a wonder, calypso an achievement, and carnival is the greatest live spectacle on earth. And all of this is true. But there is something else here, something dark, poisonous and stinking, something like a sore in this city.

It is Sunday morning. A bandy-legged, brown-skinned little man stands on the top-floor landing of the three-storeyed tenement building on Webber Street. Now he looks down. Rains earlier in the morning have left the yard wet and slippery. A woman ducks below the limp clothing hanging on a wire line, goes and opens a fowl coop. The birds reach out and try to pick the feed from her hands even before she can set it down. Four corbeaux hunched like judges on the drooping branches of the solitary coconut tree in the yard look at the dry river swollen with water and boiling with tin cans, old boots, strips of wood and other unassorted debris. Some small boys stand at the edge of the 'river' and toss bits of wood and paper in, and watch the water speed them away. In Webber Street the older boys of the neighbourhood are squared off to resume a game of football after the passing of a vehicle. But here comes the police jeep. The boys scatter. They run through yards and disappear even before the jeep comes to a stop. And now, on the other side of the street, tesses drinking in a snackette where a jukebox is blaring out a calypso walk out on the pavement, with beers in their hands, to watch the action. There is no action. The jeep stops, but the policemen are smarter than that. They do not bother to get out of the vehicle. They know from experience that they will not catch the culprits. The jeep picks up and moves off tiredly like a beaten man. The boys will come laughing from hiding now. Some of the tenants will laugh. And the tesses who had held the vain hope of seeing action will laugh and walk back in the snackette, beers still in their hands, and perhaps they will punch a livelier tune from the jukebox.

The bandy-legged little man does not laugh. He does not think it funny. It is not only that the players run the risk of being hit by a passing vehicle, not only that the football might smash a window or strike a passing woman or child (he has seen these things happen), but the behaviour of the young men. They curse drivers for going by too slowly, and show a ruthless disrespect for age and sex.

A stocky one-legged man with a thick head of hair appears from behind the building, swinging between a pair of crutches. He looks up and, seeing the bandy-legged one, calls out to him.

'Ho, Castle.'

The bandy-legged one turns and answers quickly, like he's caught off guard, 'Hello, Mr Cross.'

'What's up?'

'Nothing special. I just fixed up my bike. Just looking out before I go in.'

'How the radio playing now?'

'So-so. But you still get statics.'

'Aaah-har.' The one-legged one ponders. 'You want a new tube.'

'Can't afford that now, Mr Cross.'

'Better try and get one. Else the whole radio spoil.'

'I'll see. You know how it is.'

The one-legged one shifts, and balances on his crutches, and pulls at the place where his beard should be.

'You heard the excitement last night, Castle?'

'I was right on spot. Lucky I was alone.'

'So you know about it?'

'Yes. I was coming from the cinema. I had to run back up the road and wait till police come before I could dash upstairs. So much bottle was pelting.'

'Terrible, eh?'

'Just now decent people can't live in this place at all. Like these hooligans have no cure.'

'Police can't handle them.'

'They don't want to handle them.'

'You think so, Castle?'

'What else you want me to say? Look, Mr Cross. I have a family. My wife, my child and my little sister. Can't make it here. Can't stand this kinda living.'

'Plenty people willing to move. But where to get a place? Getting a place to rent and a job to do – two hardest things in this Trinidad.'

'Three years now I living here and this is the worst time I'm seeing now. I don't know what's wrong.'

'Too many things,' the one-legged one says.

'Mr Cross, it's like nothing is nothing… Like – I mean – like there's no meaning to anything.'

'You not wrong, Castle. But it's so all over the world. I hear is the same thing in London and the States. Is the way of the world. It's progress. Is this kind of living like there's no tomorrow. It's this great hurry, this feeling that the world going to blow itself to pieces any minute, any day. Many things involved, Castle.'

'It's damn sickening, though. You paying rent and you can't have a moment peace in this place.'

'You telling me, Castle. Is fifteen years now I here.'

'And, Mr Cross, the trouble is a man like me can't do anything about it. Only one thing – run. Pack up an' leave the place. Leave it to the hooligans.'

'Castle, I have one foot. A man can't run with one foot.'

The bandy-legged one shakes his head sadly and looks out at the street where the boys have returned and are engaged in their game of football.

'Look. You see them, Mr Cross? You see how they laughing? They don't care a damn about anything. As soon as the police gone they come back and start to kick ball. Big joke!'

Mr Cross also looks towards the street. 'Sometimes I wonder if they are to blame.'

'Who'll you blame?'

'Too many factors involved,' Mr Cross says.

The bandy-legged one thinks a while, then speaks. 'I know who to blame. Myself.'

'Yourself?'

'Yes,' the bandy-legged one says with fierce bitterness, 'I blame myself for living in this area, in this street, among these people.'

'That's one way of looking at it,' Mr Cross says.

They are silent for a moment.

'Boy, I don't know,' Mr Cross says. 'I don't know.'

Castle clears his throat and sighs as if he has already said too much.

'Well, I'm goin' in,' Mr Cross says, gripping his crutches firmly. 'I have a radio to fix for a fella this evening. When you get the tube tell me and I'll come and fix it in the radio. Okay?'

'All right, Mr Cross. I goin' in too.'

But he waits and watches the one-legged man swing off towards his place before he turns towards the door of the apartment in which he lives.

Walter walks sullenly into the living-room. The muscles above his left eye are twitching vigorously. Sometimes he gets so blasted vexed he gets a headache.

He goes into the kitchen and rests the tools with which he has been repairing his bicycle in the box under the little table, then he washes his hands and goes back into the living-room and sinks into a chair near to the radio. He hears his wife slapping pillows, cleaning out the bedroom. He turns down the volume of the radio.

'Walter?' That is his wife, making certain that it is he.

'Yeah.'

'Finish? The bike, I mean…?'

'Yes.'

'Gave you a lotta trouble?'

'No.'

'Walter?'

'Ye-es, Stephanie. It's your husband, Walter Castle. What's wrong?'

'Nothing. It's you. You sound so… so…'

'So what?'

'So… Well, you know… As if something's wrong.'

He says nothing.

'Is anything wrong?'

'Look, fer Christsake, Stephanie, what's wrong?'

He hears the deep intake of her breath, then silence. He realizes that she has stopped slapping the pillows and is wondering what is wrong with him.

'Walter?' she asks, curiously, cautiously.

'Yes, Stephanie,' he answers, patient and irritated.

'Can you put the radio on a little louder for me, please?'

'Okay.' He stretches a hand, turns the volume-control switch.

Now what? he thinks as he hears her long sigh and the sound of her slippered feet scraping from the bedroom towards him. This is a hell of a morning to wake up in. Jesus. Lord.

She enters the room and goes straight to the radio and adjusts the volume. By way of comment she adds: 'It was a little too loud and… I didn't want to bother you any more.'

Then: 'Is anything wrong?' she asks.

'Nothing… I have a headache.'

'Oh. You sounded so… Well, so… I don't know… I mean, I thought you had trouble fixing the bike. A headache?'

He doesn't answer, and she looks at him for a few long seconds.

'I'll get two pills for you. If there're any more in the bottle.' She half turns to leave, then turns and faces him. 'What's worrying you, Walter? I know something is.'

'I tell you I have a headache.'

She stands, looking wise and motherly. 'The job,' she says. 'You're thinking about the job. You're still thinking about how you didn't get the promotion you were counting on.'

'Now you telling me what I'm thinking.'

'I'm just asking, Walter. I don't know what's wrong with you this morning.'

'Is something wrong?' he asks.

'I know you,' she says. 'But it's no use worrying. You can't do anything about the job.'

'I can leave it.'

She bends her head and looks quickly at her belly swollen in pregnancy, then lifts her head and meets his gaze. 'Oh,' she says. 'Oh.'

'Oh, what?' the man challenges.

Silence settles over them. The woman makes as if to speak. No words come. She bends her head and stares at her belly.

'When a man doesn't have something to live by, he might as well be dead,' the man says.

For a while the woman looks at the wall, where there is a photograph of the two of them as bride and groom.

'What you want to do?' she asks.

'When a man's just moving, just drifting anywhere he's pushed, he's nothing,' the man says tightly, and gets up and goes by the window.

'What you want to do?'

'What can I want to do? You tell me you're having a baby.'

'And if I wasn't having the baby?'

'Nothing.'

'No. Tell me.'

'I'd pack up and leave this city, leave the job and everything,' the man says angrily.

'Where'll we go?'

'I know a place in the country.'

'And a job?'

'I can get a job.'

'You know how hard it is with jobs… Especially in the country.'

'I can get a job.'

'What kinda job?'

'President,' he says, turning around, his mouth full with anger. 'President of the Senate. Would that do?'

'You'll make me so proud.'

The man walks across the room and sits tiredly. The wife also sits.

'I bet you'll be the proudest woman in the country,' he says. 'Look, a man has to begin somewhere, some time. You can't just keep crawlin' around trying, slaving, just to stay alive so you can pay the rent and quiet the worms inside you.'

The wife sits saying nothing.

'I could get five – ten acres of land, fix up a li'l shack and go to work, plant things, rear animals. I'm not afraid of work. And things can't be worse.'

28

'Things can always be worse,' the woman says without stirring.

'But what do we have to lose? All a man – all a man really has to lose is his balls. And in this town, with hustling and bowing, your balls get squashed outa your guts so fast...'

'Patience. You must have patience, Walter.'

'Yes. Patience. I've had that for years. I'm sick with patience. Work. Keep on. Keep it up. Don't give up. Nice. You're pulling your weight. Go ahead. Nine years! Nine years I on the job. Castle do this. Castle do that. Yes, sir. All right, sir. Good. Fine. And when time for promotion, they bring a new fellow and say, Castle, this is the new officer, please give him your cooperation, and I say, Yes, sir, and teach the man the job they refuse to let me hold. Christ! A man must have some pride. That's one thing a man must have. And a man must have a point like a mule; when you reach there, you not going further. Well, I reach. I don't think I goin' back to that office in the morning.'

'Walter – '

'Wait. Listen. Girl, if a man don't have something like steel inside him that they can't touch and they can't bend, then he's a robot, something to be switched on and switched off. And, by Christ, I don't think I goin' back to work in the morning.'

'I understand,' the woman says softly. 'I understand. But the baby... In just a few months the baby...'

'No,' the man cries. 'You don't understand. You don't understand,' the man says tiredly, like he has just climbed a high hill. 'You don't understand one thing.'

'Well,' she says, a little hotly, 'you want me to tell you to leave the job?'

'You'll never say that.'

'You want me to say it?'

'Say what you want.'

'Where'll we go? You wouldn't want us to go up by your mother, and you won't go up by my father. You're too proud. You alone can't beat the world. Look at my condition! Who'll give me a job?'

'Who said anything about you working?'

'Walter,' the wife explains, like she's dealing with a stubborn child, 'you can't spite them. Darling, they're too big. You can't beat them. You think when you leave the job they'll miss you?'

'All I'm thinking is a way to get out. Get away from the job, the people and this city. That's all. Get away.'

'You'll always come into contact with people.'

'A man owns himself, and he meets people on his terms.'

'Pride. It's your pride,' she says.

'That's all a man has. Like his two balls. When he loses them he's not a man any more.'

'Well, I don't see the sense running away,' she says, softening her tone, taking a new tack.

'But you see the sense in hustling every day for… for nothing. Just eating.'

'I don't know what you want to prove, Walter.'

'Perhaps I want to prove that I'm not a blasted robot. Nine years I worked and now I get a kick in the face.'

'A lotta people get kicked.'

'Well, I don't like the feel of boots on my face.'

'You still have a wife and child.'

'Yeah. So?'

'There're times when –' the wife begins, as if what she is about to say is a hard thing, a thing difficult to put into words.

'Times when you must take your kick and grin, eh?' the man asks.

'That's not fair.'

'All right. Go ahead. There are times –'

'You have to be practical, Walter.'

'And take my kick?'

'But you can't do any better now.'

'Why?' he says hotly. 'Why not?'

'Your father shoulda been a rich man.'

'Then I wouldn't get kicked, you mean? You feel a man must subject himself to anything just to survive?'

'There's tomorrow. And we can hope for better.'

'There's no tomorrow. Every day's today. And as to hope – ! What the hell I keep wasting my breath for?'

'I'm listening,' she says.

'You hearing; you not listening.'

30

'I tell you I'm listening.'

'Okay, listen. I want to leave this place. I want to get out. We won't starve.'

'Walter, you're not sick,' the wife says. 'Say thank God for that.'

The man's voice jumps startlingly. 'Thank God for what? You really don't understand, eh? I tell you I fed up with everything around me. I'm damn well sick.'

'You need a rest.'

'I don't need no rest.'

'Sometimes people need a rest and don't know it.'

'You're a doctor now?'

'I'm not a doc… I'm just… just trying to… to help.'

'I have news for you, lady. You not helping.'

'Okay,' the wife says, tears sounding in her voice. She bends her head and folds her hands in her lap. The man, her husband, looks about the room and says Damn! under his breath. The woman brings her hands to her face and begins to cry softly. The man takes a crumbled cigarette pack from his pocket, selects a cigarette and lights it.

'Stephanie, life must mean something. Life's more than a job or a plate of food or a bed.'

'But,' the wife says, her voice trembling with tears, 'you have to wait sometimes until you get a position where you can do better. When you start with nothing, you have to work up. You have to wait.'

The man does not answer, and the wife sobs to a stop like a train arriving at the station.

'It would be better if we go away,' the man says. 'I tired waiting.'

'I don't know what to tell you again, boy.'

'I hate this stinkin' world and these rotten people,' Walter says suddenly.

'I don't think you hate the world.'

'Oh yes?'

'Yes, Walter. It's love of the world that's driving you,' she says softly, with sincerity and assurance.

'Well I like that! So I love the world, eh, darling?'

'Yes, Walter.'

'Wife of the Year,' the man says with a chuckle. 'I've just voted you Wife of the Year.'

'Thank you,' she says, attempting a smile that comes off charmingly.

'You're welcome. So I – me – Walter Castle, catching his arse since morning, love this world and these people.' He gets up and goes to the window. 'Great.'

'Walter.'

He turns and faces her, for there is urgency in her tone, and some command. 'Yes?'

'Walter, let's wait a little longer. Let's wait until the baby comes. Look, apply for leave, spend a few days away from work, and think this thing out.'

'I want to face this thing now. I want to be a man in the world. I want to be able to stand up and do what I must do.'

'You're a man, Walter.'

'But if I go back – if I haul my tail between my legs and go back, it would mean that I'm beaten. You understand?'

'You yourself told me that no one is beaten until he admits it.'

'Well, maybe I was wrong that time.'

'Then you mean you really want me to agree with you to leave and go to the country, with one baby in my hand and one inside me, without a job, on some piece of land somewhere? And what will happen to Carol?'

'You don't understand,' the man says.

'I would like to agree. For your sake I would like to agree because I feel that all this means a lot to you. But…'

'But you can't.'

'No, Walter. Not with one baby in my hand and one in my belly. I would like to agree, but…'

'Don't feel too distressed about that,' the man says with false brightness; and, without reaching the window, turns around and finds a chair.

'Walter,' she says, going to him, and in her tone asking him to try to understand her.

Tiredly, with a sense of defeat and understanding, the man reaches out a hand and touches his wife.

'You gettin' thin,' he says.

32

'You know I always get thin when I'm this way.' She sits on the arm of his chair.

Silence, apologetic and apprehensive, moves around the room.

'Stephanie?'

'Yes?'

'About this thing, this leaving. I have to think. I have to think.'

'I'll think about it too.'

'Where's Carol?'

'Gone to church.'

'Oh, I forgot.'

They sit.

'There're things… There're things that a man… that a man can't – '

'Walter. You promised to think about it.'

From the bedroom comes the sound of the baby crying.

'I better go and give her feed.'

The woman gets off the arm of the chair and moves briskly towards the room where the baby is screaming its head off. The man thinks about getting up, but doesn't; he reaches in his pocket for his cigarettes.

I have to think. I have to think…

2

So it is Sunday morning. Over the radio a preacher is preaching a sermon. You have a mental picture of a short fat man with sparse hair, false teeth, bloodshot eyes, a head cold and a rough pair of fists. 'Repent! Repent!' he shouts in his excited nasal twang; sneaking over you is the impression that he must have been married one time and his wife ran off with a sailor and he is hoping his plea to repent will reach her wherever she is.

Downstairs, the distinct beat of a motorcycle baffles into the yard; and when the motorcycle stops beating, the cheers and noises of the footballers in the street rise, and before these can fade away, a woman begins scolding a child in a high rasping key in the adjoining apartment, and then someone begins hammering on the other side and the baby, Walter's baby, begins to scream and his wife keeps saying, 'Drink the porridge, darling. Drink it. It's good for you.' But the child keeps on sputtering with its lips against the nipple of the bottle.

'Stephanie, that food is too hot,' the man calls out.

'I don't think so, Walter. I think she must have gripe.'

'Well, give her some gripe-water.'

'There isn't any more.'

'Well, give her something to make her shut up. The noise driving me outa my head.'

As if to spite him, the baby begins to scream louder. 'Now, now, now,' the mother says. 'Hush, doo-doo.' And you hear the uneven crying of the child as it is being rocked.

Jesu! This is noise! the man thinks. Wonder what's wrong with that child? Better go and see.

As soon as the man moves to get up, the child stops crying; so he sinks back into the chair, draws up the cushions like a pillow at his head, stretches out his legs and closes his eyes.

Gradually the sounds of the present fade, the world of the moment recedes, and the man finds himself plunged backwards into half-remembered days of childhood; and now he remembers the look of tall immortelle and green cocoa trees, and the scent of smoke from the wood fire in the kitchen, and the scent of wild lilies and overripe guavas at the back of the house, and the scent of camphor balls among the clothes in the bedroom. He remembers right back to the time when he was a little boy, and the evening when he went home after hunting for squirrels with his sling-shot in the cocoa, and he caught none, but there were two giant mountain doves in his dove-traps and he tied the birds and reset his traps and went home whistling like a little man.

That same evening when he reached home, he found the family packing to move, so he put the doves in a birdcage belonging to his big brother, Boysie, and went and helped them pack. He asked Boysie which part they were going to and Boysie told him they were going to Jerico, and he asked Boysie if Pap had sold the land, and Boysie told him that Pap had no land to sell. The land they were living on belonged to someone else and they had to move because Pap had given up the contract. As he didn't know what contract was, he asked Boysie and Boysie told him that contract was when one man gave another man his land to work and to bring to a proper standard of cultivation over a specified period. But, Boysie said, Pap was giving up the contract because it involved too much work and the owner got all the profit, and then, right there, Boysie said how Pap had once owned thirty-five acres of good cocoa land and had lost it all. But Boysie did not tell him how that came to happen.

And that same night they went down to Jerico with their belongings on the back of a truck. And while they were putting the things into the truck, Andrew, his other big brother, bumped the birdcage with the doves and the door flew open and the doves flew away. And when they were going down in the truck, he kept thinking about the doves that had flown away and about those that would be caught in the traps he had left in the cocoa, and how there would be no one to free them.

They went down to Jerico and he was in the back of the truck with Boysie, and Pap and Andrew were in front with the driver, because Ma and Carmen and Ruth and the little one, Chris, had travelled down by bus.

They hadn't settled in Jerico long when the thing happened with Pap. The kitchen still needed to be properly covered and there was another room to be put on to the house. It was evening and Ruth was singing a song and Carmen was in the front room hushing the baby. Boysie came straight in from the forest with his muddy boots, and Ruth, who took pride in cleaning out the house, stood and looked at him and stopped singing. And Boysie was trembling with excitement, and for a moment he didn't say a word. Then, he called Ma and when Ma came he told all about how Pap was driving the tractor in the forest and how the tractor capsized and crushed Pap's ribs and smashed his left leg and how they had rushed him to the hospital at Sangré Grande.

And Ma held her head and began to say how she didn't know what kinda man Pap was, and what kinda god God was, because Pap lost thirty-five acres of good cocoa land through drinking and merrying and whoring and he had dragged her and the children all over Trinidad, all over the countryside, wanting to work and sometimes not getting work, trying all kinda jobs, and as soon as he reached Jerico where he get a good job driving tractor he had to go and let the tractor get on top his leg and his ribs. And Ma wanted to know what she was going to do that time, with the children to feed and only Boysie doing a little work. And all of them were sad especially Ruth, Pap's favourite.

Ma and Ruth and Boysie went to see Pap at the hospital and when they came back, they told how the people at the hospital wanted to cut off Pap's foot, but Pap said no, no saw for this foot, and how he cussed the doctor and the nurses and they didn't cut the foot off.

The day Pap came out of the hospital, he looked strange and thin with the hair cut short against his scalp and his beard gone and his moustaches gone too and a pair of crutches under his armpits. The car dropped him at the roadside and went up the road to turn because the driver was afraid of skidding in the wet grass in front the house. So they let Pap out at the gap and two attendants from the hospital helped him across the yard and up the broken-down steps, and Pap was vexed that somebody had to help him. Ma stood by the door, rubbing the side of her face as if she had a beard which was scratching her, and moved aside for Pap to pass. And when Pap reached inside he sat on the nearest chair and one of the attendants from the hospital handed him a stick and Pap didn't even thank the attendants for their assistance, but he called to his wife Elizabeth. And Ma went and stood before him with her hands held across her breasts, like a little old lady out of a book, and without a word let her eyes run over him, taking in the reduction in the size of the bull neck and the chest, noting the flabbiness of the arms, and letting her gaze linger on the foot in its casing of plaster of Paris.

'Elizabeth.'

Pap's voice was soft – soft – not like the real Pap – soft and filled with fear and self-pity, and he had remained less than three months in hospital.

'Yes, Pap.'

He shook his head from side to side and his eyes filled with water. 'They wanted to cut off the foot,' he said. 'They wanted to cut off my foot.'

And his wife unfolded her arms and let them hang loosely at her sides.

'But not my foot. Not this foot!' Pap said.

And the woman, his mother, his father's wife, stood there and heaved a heavy sigh. And she did not look at Pap's eyes.

''Lizabeth,' Pap said, and looked at his foot before he looked at his wife.

'If they wanted you to cut it off, you shoulda let them, Pap.'

And his father fell silent and looked away from his wife and shook his head slowly, and water fell out of his eyes and made spots on the floor.

For days Pap sat in a chair near a window in the living-room, with the crutches on the floor beside him. He looked thinner and angrier and quieter and his foot got no better. He sat there and looked outside at the silent forest and the sky, and sometimes he turned from the window and looked about the house, at his quiet wife and the girls, Carmen and Ruth, and at Andrew and Boysie when they came from working in the forest in the evening and sat down to eat at the table, and there was sadness about Pap. And all that time there was a kind of silence about the house like a net, and a kind of anxiety in the air, as if everyone was waiting for something to happen. But what?

Carmen was the biggest girl. Whenever she had to go down the road, Ma said, 'Walter, you go with her.' But as soon as they were out of sight of the house, he took his own way and waited for her afterwards when it was time to return.

Any time there was moonlight Carmen sat on the steps and counted the stars. Sometimes Ruth and he sat with her. When it was time to sleep, Ma would call Carmen from the steps.

One night with brilliant moonlight and sparkling stars in a clear blue sky, Ruth and he left Carmen on the steps and went inside. Ruth had to mend a dress and he had to do his home lessons. Pap was reading an old newspaper that Mr Felix had lent him, and Ma sat dozing in the rocking chair.

When Ma woke out of her doze she called to Carmen, and there was no answer and Ma said nothing for a while, then got off her chair and went to the door and called again, softly, as if she didn't want Pap to hear, and still there was no answer, and none of the big boys was at home and Ma went back and sat in the rocking chair and dozed off again. When she awoke out of her doze, she called loudly for Pap to hear: 'Carmen.'

There was no answer.

'Pap, you have to talk to Carmen,' Ma said. 'You have to talk to your daughter.'

Pap pushed aside the old newspaper, prepared to listen.

'I don't know what get in she head,' the mother said. 'Look at the hour she not home!'

'What!' Pap said, and grabbed for his crutches to get up.

Ma stood and said tiredly, 'I just not able. I goin' to sleep.'

' 'Lizabeth!' Pap's voice stopped her. 'What is this? What *is* this?' The crutches were in his hands and he stamped them so hard on the floor that he was jarred off balance and fell and wouldn't let Ruth help him to his feet, but sat on his backside and shouted in a voice full with tears and anger: 'I'm a cripple. A blasted cripple!

'Lizabeth, you watch these children get on. The boys go out, come in all hours. And now, Carmen. What kinda family I have now? What kinda woman is this? Why don't you tell them something? You know all this goin' on, you do nothing to stop it and you don't tell me a damn thing.' He sat there sputtering and choking with grief and anger, and Ruth went and helped him to his feet.

And just then Carmen came in and everybody turned to look at her. And same time Andrew came in, and Pap looked at them and said, in a rough voice, 'This house is a hotel? This blasted house is a hotel? I want to know.'

And Carmen hung her head, but Andrew appeared surprised and looked at his mother, whose favourite he was, then at his father, and asked, 'What's wrong with Pap?'

And Pap heaved one of his crutches at Andrew and struck him on the knee, and Andrew said again, 'What happen to Pap?'

'You take me for a blasted cripple,' Pap said tightly.

And Andrew was going to say something, but Ma said, 'Hush, Andrew. Is not your father fault.'

After that, Pap didn't talk much. He didn't talk much when Mr Felix came over to play draughts, and he didn't talk much when Carmen began going out and coming in like she was one of the big boys, and he didn't say anything when Andrew came and said he wasn't going back to work in the forest. He didn't even look at his wife. And when he couldn't get tobacco to put in his pipe, he didn't complain. He just gripped the stem of the pipe between his teeth and bit on it; and he didn't look at his foot to see if it was ever going to heal. And the time Carmen ran off with a young man to live somewhere in San Fernando, he said nothing. He stopped playing draughts altogether and he hardly spoke to Ma and the big boys. It was after that he had fever and lay in bed for days, and Ma gave him ginger tea, and boiled karali bush for him to drink.

The time when Carmen came back home it had rained all morning, and as soon as the rain ceased Carmen appeared in front the house, with a half-shy smile on her lips, a baby in her arms, and a man at her side holding an umbrella over her head, although the rain had ceased and the sun had begun to come out. Ruth saw her and ran forward and kissed her on the cheek, and she kissed

Ruth and Ruth took the baby from her. Pap was inside sleeping. Ma came around from the kitchen and met them in the yard and stood a distance off and looked at Carmen and wiped her hands on the front of her dress because she had been washing.

'Carmen,' Ma said.

'Yes, Ma,' Carmen said. And the two of them stood looking at each other from a distance, and Carmen didn't go and kiss Ma, and Ma didn't go and kiss Carmen.

'You know your father sick?' Ma said.

And Carmen said, 'Pa? Pa sick?'

'Yes. Go inside, you'll meet him.' And Ma stood there with her head tied and the front of her dress wet, and watched Carmen and Ruth and the baby and the young man with the umbrella folded in his hands walk into the house.

Pap had just waked from sleep and was in the living-room and sat with his legs stretched out before him. It was Saturday and Boysie had gone to work and Andrew was not at home.

'Good evenin', Pap,' Carmen said.

The young man at her side said, 'Good evenin', Mr Castle.'

Pap bowed his head slowly and said, 'Good evenin', good-evenin'.'

There was silence; then Pap said, 'How are you, Carmen?'

'Well, thanks, Pap.'

And the old man shook his head forward briskly like he was keeping time to a calypso going on in his brain.

'How yuh feelin' now, Pap?' She stepped forward awkwardly and kissed Pap's forehead.

'Little better,' Pap said.

'Clem.' Carmen called to the young man with the umbrella, and he went and stood at her side before her father. 'Pap, this is Clem,' Carmen said.

'Mitchell,' the young man said and stretched out his hands to grasp Pap's. Then he went and took a seat and Carmen also sat down, but Ruth went with the baby in her arms and stood near to Pap's chair.

'We're gettin' married, Pap,' Carmen said.

Pap held his nose between two fingers and said nothing.

'Pap,' Carmen appealed softly. 'Pap – '

40

'You coulda done things different,' the old man said.

Carmen bent her head as if she was looking to see if her clothes were fitting well. 'Yes, Pap,' she said in a small voice. 'Pap, I... We sorry, Pap.'

'I's your father now and I was your father that time.'

'We sorry, Pap.'

'Better we don't talk about that,' Pap said. 'Who are you, young man?'

And the young man told Pap who he was.

'How you making out?' Pap asked the young man.

'Okay,' the young man said.

'Clem is a mechanic,' Carmen offered.

'Mechanic,' the old man echoed. 'Good.'

'And I drive truck sometimes,' the young man added.

'What's the baby's name, Carmen?' Ruth asked.

'Robinson, Robinson Everad,' Carmen said, with a mixture of pride and shyness.

Ruth held up the baby before Pap and Pap put his big clumsy fingers under the child's neck, and when the infant laughed Ruth said, 'Look! He's laughing with Pap.'

'You know he resemble Pap,' Ruth said.

'Yes,' Carmen agreed.

'Call your mother,' Pap commanded.

'Go and call Ma, Walter,' Ruth said. And he went and called Ma, who was outside washing.

Ma came in and was introduced to the young man, and she looked at the baby, and when Ruth repeated how the baby resembled Pap, Ma agreed; then excused herself and went outside because she wanted to finish washing to catch the sun that had come out.

And after they had talked with Pap and Ruth and were about to leave, Carmen and Clem asked to see Ma and Ma came. They shook hands and Carmen kissed Pap and Ma, kissed everybody, and Clem shook hands all around. Ruth and he walked with them to the road and Carmen gave him a shilling.

When the big boys came home, Pap called them into the living-room.

'Your sister was here today,' the old man said.

41

Boysie said, 'Carmen?'

'Yes, and she brought the fellow. She have a baby.'

Andrew cleared his throat.

'She's getting married,' Pap said. 'She wants Ruth and you boys to go to the wedding.'

'All right, Pap,' Boysie, the elder, said.

'And you, Andrew?'

Andrew was looking at a spot on the ceiling.

'What about you, Andrew? Andrew!'

Andrew brought his eyes down slowly and looked before him, but not at Pap. 'I not goin', Pap,' he said.

Boysie turned and looked at Andrew and Pap stirred in his chair. Andrew was the third child, the one after Carmen. He had applied to join the police force and was expecting to be called at any time.

Pap looked from Andrew to Boysie.

'I will go, Pap,' Boysie said quickly.

'Andrew!' Pap said. 'Don't talk stupidness. Don't talk foolishness to me. Why? Why?'

'I don't feel to go, Pap.'

'Boy, boy, boy,' the old man said. 'Get away from me.'

The boys left, Andrew hurrying out first, and Boysie, lingering to see if there was anything he could do for his father, bent forward in the chair and squeezing his head with both hands.

'I shoulda let them cut off the blasted foot,' Pap said.

And for days Pap was angry, and he was angrier still some months after, when Carmen was married and Boysie and Ruth brought home some of the wedding cake. But when Andrew was offered, he refused to eat, saying he didn't like wedding cake.

It was just approaching dusk and Ruth was about to clean the shade of the kerosene lamp, and Pap said, 'Ruth, hand 'im the cake!' And Ruth took the saucer with the cake and carried it to Andrew, who was right there in the living-room.

'Boy,' Pap said in a clear, unemotional voice, 'you either eat this cake or find somewhere to sleep tonight.'

And Andrew looked at his father and saw that he meant business, just like the Pap of old, before the accident with the tractor. Then he took the piece of cake and bit it, and Pap sat right there and watched him eat it all.

'You're no judge of the world,' Pap said, as if he was sorry for Andrew; and picked up his crutches and went into the bedroom.

When the letter came telling Andrew that he had been selected for training as a policeman, Ma said, 'Thank you, Jesus.'

Andrew left home and went down to St James Barracks to train. The first day he came home after that, it had been raining, and he had a cloak on over his uniform. When he took the cloak off, Walter saw how shiny were his buttons, but his new leather belt was too new to take the polish well. Pap was lying down in the bedroom and Andrew walked through the house, so his boots thumped loudly on the wooden floor.

'Who the hell makin' that racket?' Pap called out.

Andrew stepped towards the room – proud Andrew that had scorned to go to the wedding of his own sister, that everyone said took after his mother. Andrew stepped towards the room and said, 'I, Pap.'

'That's damn nice,' Pap said. 'Carry on.' But Andrew didn't carry on.

There were days Walter saw his father's face pleated with many sorrows and strained with an anger that was expressed in puzzled, frustrated silence directed at himself and his invalidity rather than at anyone or anything else. Those were the days when his thin, silent mother went about the house with an air of bewilderment and surrender and old wisdom, as if she knew when she would die and where she would go to when she did. There were a few times when her eyes would light up at sight of Andrew, stiff and grave in his grey shirt and blue serge pants and his black cap with the peak shining – the uniform of the Trinidad Police Force – but these were few indeed to the times when she would look at her husband, beaten and brooding as he sat in his chair with his legs stretched out and his crutches on the floor beside him, or when she looked at Boysie, mud-spattered, tired and wet from a day in the forest.

The goat was bawling outside because one of the children had hit it with a stone. It was a quiet afternoon otherwise. Ma burst into the living-room choking with rage too big for her to hold. It was the first time Walter had seen his mother so warmed up. Ruth came behind her, dragging her feet and covering her face with her hands. Pap straightened in his chair when he saw them coming. It was a chilly day, Pap wasn't feeling well, so he had an old jacket thrown around his shoulders.

'Go and stand up in front your father,' Ma said. Her voice was tight and sharp.

Ruth obeyed slowly, her hands still covering her face.

'What?' Pap wanted to know.

'This is your daughter,' the mother said

'This is your daughter! Look! Look at her!'

Pap ran his eyes over Ruth's body, and he didn't say a word. Then he turned away and after a moment turned and looked at her again; that time, he let his eyes linger on her belly. He looked away.

'Look at her!' the mother commanded. And the old man looked at Ruth, his favourite child.

'Ruth,' Pap said softly.

Ruth stood before him, with her hands hiding her face.

'Ruth!' And the lash of Pap's voice startled Ruth so that she trembled where she stood.

'Yes, Pap,' she answered through her fingers, in a voice muffled with sorrow and fright.

Ma stood with her arms akimbo and her face a mask, and breathed heavily.

'Ruth,' Pap groaned.

'That is your daughter,' Ma said.

And the girl ran forward and fell upon her father's shoulder and began to sob as if her heart would break.

'Pap, Pap, Pap,' she cried, stifling with tears. And the old man patted her on the back to comfort her. Then she began relating the story.

It was a teacher in the school. He loved her. He wanted to marry her. But his father was opposed to the marriage. Oh God, she was sorry! She could kill herself for bringing such shame on the family. More shame after the shame Carmen had brought. She could drown herself in the river over by the sawmill. Oh Lord, she didn't know what to do. Pap, Pap, Pap.

And Ma looked on, furious and grim, her gaze accusing them

both: the daughter for her sin, and the father for comforting the child.

When Boysie came home from work, Pap told him about it and asked him to bring the young man to him.

Some days later, a thin young man with close-cropped hair appeared at the gap and walked up to the door and knocked. Pap was alone in the living-room and the young man went in. Pap and he spoke for a long time and then he left.

Not long after, a tall thin man in a brown suit drove a car up to the front of the house, got out and went straight up to the front door and knocked. Ma let him in and called Pap from the bedroom to speak to him. Nobody heard what was said until Pap's voice rose loud and furious: 'Get out, mister! Get out!' There was the whack of a stick and an animal grunt of bare fury from the old man. Then the man in the brown suit rushed out, holding his head, and went straight to his car and drove away at a great speed, his tyres skidding and crying as the car turned and shot down the street.

When everybody rushed inside, Pap was lighting his pipe with trembling hands, and on his face was a mark of anger and justification – the sign of readiness for battle.

'You strike the man, Papito?' Ma asked.

'Yes. I strike the man.'

'It was the boy father, eh, Papito?'

'Yes. It was the boy's stupid father.'

Ma didn't say anything more to Pap, but when Andrew came for the weekend she told him that Pap was wrong to strike the man when all the man did was to say that his son would see that the baby Ruth was carrying would be well taken care of.

'And what about Ruth, Ma?'

'They were going to see the baby got everything,' Ma said.

'Was the boy goin' to marry Ruth, Ma?'

Ma didn't bother to answer that.

That was one time Walter was proud of his father. He was proud of his old man although his hair was tangled and greying, although he had fêted and whored and drunk away thirty-five acres of good cocoa land that his father had left him, and had dragged his family across the country districts of the island while he looked for work, and when he did get a steady job driving tractor, pulling logs from the forest, he had been fool enough to get himself under the wheel. There were many times he had pitied his father, and there were times he had been angry with him, but that time he was proud.

The thin young man with the close-cropped hair called again and spoke with Pap, and Pap called Ma and Ruth and they all talked and there was laughter coming from the living-room. When the young man was leaving, Ruth walked to the gap with him and he looked back and waved to her and she waved back to him as he went down the road.

Ma told Mrs Palmer that it would be a small, quiet wedding. Pap told Boysie that they would have to fix up the steps of the house, at least. Andrew said he would get a new suit. Ruth said she didn't care if the dress didn't keep her tummy down. Mr Felix said that Mr Ramroop and he could help build a tent in the yard.

The day they were building the tent, a policeman brought a summons for Pap to appear as defendant in a case of assault on the person of Osborne Hamilton. Mr Felix read the summons and said that Pap should take a lawyer. Boysie also agreed that Pap should take a lawyer. Pap said that he had no money for lawyer, and even if he had the money he wouldn't waste it on a matter like that. Pap asked Ruth to put his grey suit out in the sun. That was the only preparation he made for the case. When Andrew came up that weekend, he too tried to persuade Pap to take a lawyer. Pap refused.

The day before the case was called Mr Felix and Pap sat in front the house, playing a game of draughts.

'Castle, you're a fool,' Mr Felix said. 'You should take a lawyer.'

'I'm a poor man, Felix.'

'That's why you's a fool.'

'I don't understand you, Felix.'

'The man you hit is a civil servant, a big man. He wouldn't take you to court unless he think he could win you.'

'Well, everybody have feelings, but the law is the law, and justice is justice.'

'You think so? You think they goin' to believe you or that man?'

'Maybe they'll believe the truth.'

'The truth depends on who say it.'

'I can't afford to believe that, Felix.'

'That's why I tell you you's a fool. You can't fight that man without lawyer.'

'They have laws in this country for everybody, and a man is a man, and if a man can't stand up when he's right, when could he stand up, Felix? When?'

'I hope you right, Castle.'

Boysie didn't go to work on the day of the case. He helped Pap into the taxi. All the neighbours were there looking out to see Pap in his grey suit. When Pap came back, he took off his jacket and said: 'I told Felix that there's laws for everybody in this country, but I wonder if I'm right.'

'They charged you, Pap?' Ruth asked.

'Fifteen shillings,' Pap said, 'for being a man.'

Ruth got married. The neighbours were there: Mrs Palmer and Mr Felix and Mr Ramroop and his wife and his big daughter, Rookmin; and some of Andrew's friends and a few of Lester's friends, the teachers from the school. Everybody said that Ruth made a lovely bride. Pap made a speech and Ruth wanted to cry. Everybody agreed that she wanted to cry. Mr Felix got drunk and begged to be allowed to play his quattro. Mr Ramroop got drunk and cried; his wife and his big daughter Rookmin carried him home. The same night Ruth and her husband Lester travelled down to Port of Spain because they had rented an apartment at Belmont, since Lester had been transferred from Jerico. That ended that.

'Walter,' Pap said, one evening. 'Where you going?'

Walter had just come from school and was actually going to untie the goat and carry it to graze Mr Ramroop's hibiscus hedge. He told Pap where he was going.

'You mind if I come with you?'

'No, Pap.'

Walter waited until his father had gathered his crutches. They walked slowly. Walter walked among the weeds and left the track for his father.

'You not goin' to graze it on Ramroop fence?' Pap wanted to know.

'Not on the fence, Pap.'

'Good.'

He untied the goat, and they walked towards Mr Ramroop's hibiscus hedge.

'You growing fast,' Pap said.

Walter said nothing.

'The boys and I talk. We think you should leave this school and go to high school.'

Walter made no comment.

'You know, it's a funny thing about life.'

'What, Pap?'

'All a man get from it is experience.' Pap laughed. 'And a man needs experience to get him through it.'

Walter laughed because his father had laughed.

'But my experience,' Pap said, 'is my experience. You have to get yours yourself. You know, boy, there's a lot to learn. You learn that you're just a man.' (Pap spoke as if to himself.) 'A man is the greatest thing in God's earth, and a man is the weakest thing in God's earth. You learn to turn around and laugh at yourself. You shouldn't take yourself too seriously. You little and weak, you afraid and you get angry. And you should not hold yourself too casually because you're man.'

They reached Mr Ramroop's hibiscus hedge and the boy gave the goat freedom among the railway daisies and carpenter's grass, but held it away from Mr Ramroop's fence because his father was present. Pap searched around for a place to sit and found a large tree-stump and sat down.

'I'm just a bee with a broken wing,' Pap said. He said it too sadly. 'I can't work and am not one of the drones that doesn't have to work. You know about bees, boy?'

'Not much, Pap.'

'Well, let me tell you.'

And his father sat there and told him all about bees: about the workers and the drones and the queen; and how the workers did all the work and how the queen laid eggs and how all the drones did was to drink honey and mate the queen and then fall dead.

'What makes the workers want to work so, Pap?'

'Maybe they just can't help it. Maybe it's instinct, like a man wanting to live on, no matter how hard life is with him.'

'But why workers do all the work and drones none, Pap?'

'Workers are workers and drones are drones, boy. And I don't know which is better off.'

'I'd prefer to be a bird, Pap.'

Pap laughed and stood up because the goat was filled and the sky was getting red where the sun was sinking.

'A bee can't be a bird, boy,' Pap said.

Birds flitted about and a few butterflies zig-zagged with deliberate ease.

Pap said, 'You know something, Walter? I have one thing to tell you, and still I'm not sure if I'm right. But I think I am… Yes. I am. You have to have laws to live by.'

'Government laws, Pap?'

'Yes, government laws, and your own laws too. You have to have laws.'

They walked back to the yard and he kept thinking of bees and birds and butterflies, and of how Pap had chosen to speak to him that time, and how it would be in high school.

The school term had ended some weeks previously. He was standing before his father. Boysie and Andrew were there. He had on a short pants and a pair of dirty sneakers.

Andrew looked at him and said, 'I never seen you looking tidy, Walter.'

He looked down at his dirty sneakers and made no comment.

'We sendin' you to high school. Not to skylark: to learn,' Andrew said.

Boysie said, 'He know that, Andrew.'

'I never had the opportunity, neither Boysie,' Andrew said. 'If I had the opportunity… If I had, I don't know what I might have been.'

'A doctor,' Walter said. 'You'd have been a doctor.'

The old man smiled. That silenced Andrew.

'Well, what do you say?' Pap said.

They all looked at him, as if they were afraid he would say no.

He really wanted to say no, not because he didn't want to go to high school, but because he didn't want to feel indebted to Andrew for contributing to his going.

49

He looked at his father, he looked at Boysie, he looked at Andrew. He nodded. 'Yes, Pap.'

'Good,' his father said. 'Good.'

When the new term began, he didn't go back to primary school where he had always been fighting; fighting almost every Friday after school and never winning a fight, because he never fought with boys his size; always the bigger boys, always the boys of whom the others were afraid; but fighting all the same, and sometimes getting in a good punch and busting a fellow's mouth, or stopping a fellow's wind; but those times were rare, and more often than not he would have to run by the standpipe and wash his hurting face and fix his clothes before he walked home with his books tucked in the waist of his pants. When the new term began, he didn't go back to that school, he went to high school, to the town about seven miles from Jerico. He was wary and watchful that time.

At school, he was puzzled and sometimes outspoken and self-opinionated to the point of actual conceit. He lost friends much faster than he made them, and wondered why everybody was against him, why they all had to argue with him, why he couldn't just be one of the boys instead of being picked on and made to look foolish. He was very lonely that time, and there was no one to whom he could take his troubles. There was no one that would understand – not even Boysie, because that time Boysie had his own unhappiness to cope with; and Ruth wasn't at home, and he didn't like to talk to Pap about those things, and talking to Ma or to Andrew was out of the question.

And then Boysie went away too. Good old Boysie; strong, responsible Boysie; robust Boysie, who used to drive a tractor in the forest, like Pap; Boysie who used to smile at everything as if he were an idiot. One day Boysie came, speaking in a confused, stammering manner, as if he were telling a lie, Boysie came and stood before Pap and told him that he was going to England.

It was evening time. The last rays of sunlight streamed in through the open window on the western side of the room and rested on Pap's face. He was sitting in a corner reading a book, and

Pap said, 'Walter, please pull in that window for me.' And he went and pulled in the window.

Pap turned to Boysie. 'You were saying…?' Pap said.

'I'm goin' England, Pap.'

'You?'

'Yes, Pap. I have everything arranged. I'm goin' next two weeks.'

'Why didn't you wait until two days before, or two hours before telling me?'

The old man's reproach was so skilful and his tone so mild that for a moment Boysie was caught.

'I wasn't certain, Pap,' Boysie apologized.

'Well,' his father said. And he raised his eyes and steadied his shoulders like he was a military man facing execution and being brave and stiff and almost proud; raising his eyes, steadying his shoulders and saying, 'All right. Fire!'

'You'll have to take care of yourself, son.'

'Pap,' Boysie said. 'I've been with you for a long time. I worked in the forest for a long time.'

'You work hard. Don't say nothing else.' Pap sat erect like a bag of propped-up rice paddy and his eyes showed not hurt, not anger, but resignation, just like the eyes of a deer he had once seen. They had chased the deer for three hours – Mr Felix and Boysie and he – and it had given the dogs a good run, and when it reached the point of exhaustion, it stopped, turned and looked at its pursuers, making no real effort either to defend itself or to turn to attack. Pap's eyes looked just like that deer's eyes, that time.

'Pap,' Boysie said, 'I have a girl. She goin' England. I love the girl, Pap. I have to go.'

'You worked hard, Boysie.'

'I don't want to leave, but I must.'

'Go,' the old man said. 'Go and tell your mother.'

'Told her already,' the son said.

'Well, go and tell the others. Go.'

Boysie stood, turned, hesitated. 'Pap,' he began, as if he wanted something from his father.

'Go,' the old man said. 'You didn't make the world.'

And when Boysie dragged himself off, Pap shut his eyes tightly and shook his head like he wanted to get rid of something sticking in his brain.

At the wharf many people stood around saying goodbye: some kissed, some waved, some shook hands, some embraced, some stood at a distance and no words left their lips, some spoke with their eyes, and the eyes of some were clouded with tears.

The sky was overcast and Andrew kept looking at a fellow who was saying, 'It's goin' to rain. It's goin' to rain.'

When the fellow saw Andrew looking at him, he said, 'You think it'll rain, pardner?'

'I don't think so,' Andrew said. 'At least not until the ship leaves.'

The guards let Andrew help Boysie put his luggage aboard because Andrew was wearing his police uniform and knew the guard.

When they were finished putting the luggage on board, Boysie came back with Andrew, and the three brothers stood, not knowing what to say.

Boysie said, 'This time now, if I in the forest, I done make two trips with the tractor and going back for my third.'

Andrew said, 'Where you goin' now, you wouldn't touch a tractor.'

A slow spread of sorrow crossed Boysie's face. 'Only Ma and Pap and the children home now,' he said.

'Yes,' Andrew said.

Walter grinned, nodded and said, 'Yes.'

Andrew said, 'He's goin' to be a short man. Take after his father.'

'You goin' to make out, eh, Andrew?' Boysie asked.

'Yes,' Andrew said.

'And Walter, you'll have to take care of the folks when Andrew not there.'

Walter smiled and Andrew said, 'He's a big man of fifteen now.'

'You don't think I run out on you, eh, Andrew?' Boysie said.

'How you could want me to think that, Boysie.'

'You know everything on your shoulders now, and I goin' England.'

'What you have to make yourself miserable for?' Andrew said. 'Suppose was jail you was goin' to.'

Boysie laughed and Andrew laughed and he laughed.

'Well, you-all will write when I write you, eh?'

'As fast as you write,' Andrew said.

'Okay.'

Passengers were getting aboard. Boysie hugged his two brothers then went aboard. Andrew went with him because he was wearing his police uniform and knew the guard.

When Andrew returned, he stood next to Walter and they looked at Boysie on the deck. It was that time the water had come spilling from his eyes and a tenderness had arisen in his heart for his big brother Boysie. He had pushed back the tears because he didn't want people to see him crying.

'Boysie gone now,' Andrew said, without looking at Walter.

'Yes, he's gone.'

'Well, let's go. I have to get back to work. I only asked for an hour off.'

That time they waved to Boysie up on the deck of the ship, then turned and left because Andrew had to go to take up duty, although the ship had not left the harbour.

Then it was a Sunday. It was his birthday and he had received no presents. He was sitting in the yard under the plum tree, looking at a cockfight between Mr Ramroop's red-and-white cock and Pap's one-eyed, clean-neck cock, and his mother came up. And in her bored, lazy, sing-song said: 'Walter, why don't you chase those cocks away. They will kill one another, boy.'

He took up a stone and flung it casually between the two birds, and when they refused to separate, he went between them and chased them – Sh-shh! Sh-shhh! And they separated a few paces and stood eyeing each other.

'Yuh father say he feel to eat chicken today,' Ma said.

'Which one, Ma?'

He stood, ready and eager to catch the unfortunate bird. All he had to do was to make a slippery knot on a piece of twine, spread the twine out in a circle, throw some feed in the circle, whistle the fowls and wait for the marked bird to stand in the circle.

'The big cock,' Ma said.

'The big cock, Ma?'

'Tha's what yuh father say. Kill the big cock and invite Mr Felix for lunch. And send some for Mrs Palmer and Mr Ramroop.'

'But Ma…'

'I know we was saving the big cock for Christmas. But yuh father say kill it. So don't stand there with yuh mouth hanging open. Go and get some corn and call the fowls.'

'Awright, Ma.'

That day they killed the big cock and it nearly couldn't hold in the big iron pot. Ma was sorry that Andrew wasn't home that time, but Walter was not sorry because Andrew's absence caused his share to be increased.

Mr Felix came over for lunch. When they were finished eating, Mr Felix went home for his quattro and also brought a flask of Mountain Dew. And he and Pap drank and played, and afterwards Mrs Palmer and Mr Ramroop came and joined them. And they sang old Spanish songs, and Pap grew merry that time and wanted Ma to give him a kiss, but Ma was ashamed because Mrs Palmer and Mr Ramroop and Mr Felix were present.

Mrs Palmer said, 'Elizabeth, kiss the man nuh, girl.' But Ma wouldn't kiss him.

And that whole evening the neighbours remained talking and singing and playing quattro, even when the flask of Mountain Dew was finished. And they danced, and everybody wanted to see Mr Ramroop dance because he danced in the awkward East Indian fashion, a waltz, a castilliane or a calypso.

Pap couldn't dance; he bent his head and played the quattro.

That was the same night his mother came into the room where he slept. She was quiet so as not to awaken the two small children sleeping near by.

'Walter.' She shook him, and he awoke drunk and silly with slumber. 'Walter!'

'Mmm?'

'Walter. Listen to me. Put on this old jacket and put on your shoes and go by Mr Felix and by Mr Ramroop and Mrs Palmer. Tell them Pap dead.'

He was silly with slumber and he didn't grasp exactly what she was saying. Then, when he was out of bed and feeling in the darkness under the bed for his shoes, it struck him what she had said.

'What you say, Ma?'

'Pap dead. Yuh father dead,' she said, as if she was reporting the most ordinary occurrence. 'Don't worry to cry now. Go quick. And call Mr Felix and Mr Ramroop and pass by Mrs Palmer. Don't make too much noise.'

Outside the moonlight was shining softly upon the trees and there were huge shadows on the road, and he was thinking that that was not a night on which his father should die.

He went by Mr Felix first and the dogs were barking, and he stood in the road for a long time before he went and called Mr Felix. Mr Felix wanted to know who the hell it was at that hour of night. So he told Mr Felix what had happened and Mr Felix cursed the dogs, making noise in the road, then went and changed his clothes.

Mr Ramroop was sleeping, but his wife heard the dogs barking and when he called, she came to the door, and when he told her what had happened, she bawled, 'Oh Lawd! Neighbour!' and went inside to wake her husband. He left and went down the road by Mrs Palmer. The moon went behind some clouds and the road was dark and he began to remember that his father was dead and he began to cry, and he stumbled and fell down in the gutter before Mrs Palmer's house, and the dogs came sniffing and snarling about him, then they began to fight among themselves and he got out the gutter and ran right up to the front door of Mrs Palmer's house and knocked loudly and cried out that his father was dead and that Ma wanted Mrs Palmer to come over right away. Mrs Palmer didn't open the door. She kept saying, 'Who is that? You, Walter? What happen? Papito dead? You lie.' And he had to tell her over and over again, and then, he didn't tell her any more because the tears were in his eyes and at the corners of his lips and he felt like there was sawdust stuffed in his throat.

That very night Mr Felix took his bicycle and rode down to the village where there was a telephone booth and telephoned Andrew and gave him the news; and later the police jeep dropped Andrew home.

They buried Pap the following day. The family were all together. The last time they were together at one time and at one place. The mother, in a black dress and black hat, looked shrunken and frightened like a witch about to be burnt; the little ones, Carol and Chris, like Hansel and Gretel, stood around her as if they did not belong to her, but had strayed and been lost and were just standing near that woman, waiting for their real parents to appear and claim them. Ruth was there with her husband, Lester; but Carmen's husband couldn't come up from Point Fontin where he was working. Carmen was there. And Andrew, head of the family that time, standing with his head slightly bent, not looking at any of them, standing a little apart, as if he were ashamed to lift his eyes and accuse them or be accused by them, standing there in the cemetery after they had buried Pap as if he had been sent from another land to take care of those poor unfortunate people, and as if no ties of common blood bound him to them.

'Man that is born of a woman is of few days and full of trouble,' the preacher said, as if he knew what he was saying, as if he had known Papito Castle and the life he had led.

The cemetery was muddy, and he walked through the mud with his shoes. When he reached home, he went behind the house and sat on a pile of lumber that had been bought to repair the house, and there stifled, not so much with grief as with anger, and he kept thinking about how just the day before Pap had ordered Ma to kill the big cock and how Pap had played Mr Felix's quattro and had drunk the Mountain Dew and sung old Spanish songs and hadn't raised his head to look at Mr Ramroop dance; and how he had asked Ma to give him a kiss, and how Ma was ashamed because Mrs Palmer was there and Mr Ramroop and Mr Felix, and how Mrs Palmer had said, 'Elizabeth, kiss the man nuh, girl.' And how Ma still hadn't kissed him; and he wondered why his father had to die.

It wasn't so long after Pap's death that Walter came from the village football ground, mud-spattered and wet after a game. Andrew had come home for the weekend. He met him in the yard, right there by the plum tree.

'But Walter,' Andrew said, 'I don't see you picking up a book.

I don't see you studying. Like you don't realize what's happening. Boysie gone England, Pap dead, and everything on my shoulders now. Like you don't realize.'

He was wet down, and as the wind blew he grew chilly and the cold bumps swelled on his skin. 'I want to go and change my clothes, Andrew,' he said.

'I'm talking to you, boy!'

'Andrew, I'm wet and it's cold. I want to go and change my clothes.'

'Now look, boy! Don't get rude with me.'

'But, Andrew –'

'Wet or no wet, cold or no cold, you'll stand and listen.'

'Well, I'm goin' to change my clothes.'

He had walked off and left his brother standing. He had never got on well with Andrew, although it was he that paid his school fees. Perhaps it was because he paid them grudgingly, like a man who gives charity, then expects the beggar to fall on his knees and kiss his feet in thanks.

Later, in the house, Andrew was speaking to their mother.

'Ma, I don't know what to say to that boy Walter at all. I just don't understand him. Maybe it's better he leave high school. I don't know if high school doing him any good.'

'Anything you say, Andrew,' Ma said.

'And he's rude on the back of it. I am trying to help the boy and he's rude. Look at him now!'

He had been entering the room that time, and, hearing the last remark, had sucked his teeth. Before he could turn back, Andrew called him.

'What you say, boy?' Andrew asked.

'Nothing.'

'You think you's man or what, Walter?'

He hadn't answered.

'Answer me!' Andrew said.

He didn't answer, and his mother turned her hands over in her lap in a sign of resignation; and Andrew began to get real vexed.

'This won't do! This won't do at all. Maybe it's better I take you outa high school.'

'Walter, why don't you answer your brother?' Ma said.

But he had nothing to say. What could he answer and say?

'Your father is dead,' Andrew said, beginning a lecture.

That time the anger came over Walter, and there were no words he could utter. Tears had come to his eyes and he had turned and run out of the room.

There was a new moon and the ground was damp and he ran, ran into the night filled with the sounds of mating frogs, and crickets and twinkling with candle-flies; he ran until the wind caught in his side and his chest was fit to burst, ran down the track near the river, over by the sawmill, and he was crying as he ran, and blowing the snot from his nostrils without stopping; and when his legs were tired and the muscles in his thighs felt stiff and lumpy, he stopped and wiped the tears and the perspiration from his face with the tail of his shirt. Then he threw himself down on the soft dust-pile by the sawmill, panting hard and angry, and a candle-fly came and lit on his knee, and his hands swooped down to crush it, but in that moment his anger at the fly faded, and he thought, Look at you! You come to light the night and you find yourself under my hand. Go way! Go way! He held the fly and flung it into the night. If I was you I would just fly straight out this goddam world. But the fly came right back and settled on the front of his shirt, and he thought, You're a fool. A damned fool. But he let it alone and lay there thinking that it was time for him to leave home and strike out on his own.

And when he had control of himself, he stood, dusted his clothes and walked home slowly, telling himself that he would leave home, leave school and go out on his own, and he believed all that he told himself that time.

It was his last day at school. No one knew, because he had told no one. Peter Mailey was the captain of the football team. He came and sat next to Walter during the period after lunch.

'Castle, I hear you can play football,' Mailey said. 'How come you never come to practice with the boys?'

'You-all never ask me. You ask everybody else, but you never ask me.'

'Oh shit, man! We never ask anybody,' Mailey said uncomfortably. 'Fellas just come up and play and see if they can make the side. What position you play?'

'Inside left.'

'You could come and practise this evening?'

'I can't come.'

'What happen?'

'I'm leavin' school. I'm not coming back.'

'You mean… you leavin'… school?'

'Yes. Leavin'. You bitches must be happy, eh?' he said. He had been angry and didn't care what he said.

'I'm not happy, man. Sorry, and I sure the others sorry too. Leavin' school…' Peter Mailey said, wondering.

Afterwards Peter Mailey whispered to the boys in the same row that Castle was leaving school, and soon it was whispered through the form; and the fellows were sorry. The same fellows with whom he used to fight and row were sorry and they said so – not with words, for these didn't come easily to them, but they came up and looked at him and tried to speak of some past incident, and they seemed to feel grieved that they didn't have any words. And he felt sorry too, not only because he was leaving school, but because he had always thought that the fellows were just a pack of bitches; but he said nothing, for he himself had no words.

He left school. He was sixteen, and that time he felt soft and awkward inside, especially about the boys at school. When he slipped away from the house that night, he left a note for his mother, but the note was really for Andrew. He took a taxi and went down by Ruth, who had a place at Belmont, and he slept there that night, on the couch in the living-room, because the place was small with only one bedroom, and afterwards Lester, Ruth's husband, arranged for his aunt to give him a little room at another place. Lester gave him a cot and he put it in the room. That ended that; rather, it began something.

He went looking for work. There were so many signs in the city. There were big signs with big black letters, and some had red letters; and there were small signs, almost hidden, so you saw them only after you had tucked your shirt in at your waist and were swallowing the spittle in your throat until you felt it was your Adam's apple you were swallowing – after you had done that and had rubbed the sweat from the palms of your hands and were mounting the steps of the building, thinking what you were going to say when you got into the office, you saw one: 'No Vacancy', it said, or simply, 'No Hands'; and there was one witty firm with one 'Don't Bother To Knock' tacked on to the door marked 'Enquiries'; and it wasn't hard to tell what they meant, or to whom they spoke. You saw those signs and you felt your spirits drop, and you kept thinking how you had walked the city for the whole day, and how your feet were killing you and your shoe soles were getting thinner and thinner, and how you were a man in the world, and wondered how was a man ever going to stand up as a man if he couldn't get something to put his hands to – if he wasn't given the opportunity to be that man. And you thought about Marilyn Monroe and the amount of dollars she received for making the movie *Don't Bother To Knock* and you thought of Humphrey Bogart with a gun in his fists, and you thought how he was just play-acting, and how a man could be driven to point a gun for real, and he didn't need to have a voice like Humphrey Bogart's.

You thought of school you had just left, and the fellows you had left there, and you thought of Andrew. There are many Andrews in the world, but you thought of your own individual Andrew, with his silver buttons polished and shining and his belt and the peak of his cap polished and shining too, and you thought of Ma and you wanted to groan, and you thought of Pap, and how he used to sit, a cripple in his chair, tired and angry, pretending that he was not beaten; and you thought of the million other fellows like yourself, little fellows, little men that figured they could get through, that figured they could make a dent in the armour of the giant, and you thought of the giant with his big hands and his rough voice, and you wondered where, in the midst of all this, was God.

You saw the signs, those hung up and those placed against a wall, for you to see. You saw signs in the way people spoke and in the way they hurried, and you saw signs in the eyes of some; and sometimes just the way a man smiled was a sign.

'What you want, sonny?' The man smiled faintly, and you got the sign already; still, you said, 'I'm looking for a job, sir.' And you looked at his lips. 'What kinda job, son? What can you do?'

In your mind you thought, What can I do? What can I do? 'Any type of job, sir, any...' And you watched how he looked at you carefully like you're a mangy stray dog he's about to purchase from the dog-catchers. 'Too small,' he said finally. And you wanted to smash something to save you going crazy.

That time Walter was so hungry and broke that he wanted to cry, but he couldn't afford to waste the tears, so he walked the city streets slowly, slowly, sometimes with his head bent, looking at the ground, hoping he would find a dollar, or even a shilling, finding none, but walking with his head bent never the less, because it is the portion of youth to hope and to be disillusioned in time. He learnt that later, that and much more.

He walked through Port of Spain, and sometimes the sun was so hot, and the crowds so thick that the place seemed to give off steam; and he walked under the eaves of buildings, in the shade, going about the business of seeking employment, quietly as a beaten dog, only he wasn't beaten, to his little room, the room slightly bigger than a fowl coop; went through the door and threw himself on the cot and fell asleep with all his clothes on, hungry.

Sometimes he went over by Lester's aunt and she gave him some food, but as the days went by, such visits decreased in frequency because his pride refused to allow him to be a consistent beggar.

Three months, then he managed to get a job. And it was as if it had been three long years. But he got the job as office boy, and the boss was an angry man, given to moods during which he would shout 'Boy!' He would shout 'Boy!' so that Walter used to feel the hair rise on his neck as if he were a fox-terrier challenged to fight, and the grief reached to his throat but never to his eyes. 'Boy,' Mr Calix would shout, and he would go sullenly and would render whatever service was required.

Three months he was on that job, and it was as if it had been three weeks. Three months, and then he was back on the city, dumped into the stream of the insecure and unemployed, pounding the pavement, enquiring here and enquiring there, and sometimes not enquiring at all, but going up to the Public Library, upstairs where there was a sign 'Quiet Please', going up there and reading book after book after book until he was too hungry or too fatigued to read more.

Then there was one odd job after another: working in a gas-station, working at a drugstore owned by a fat woman, working in a shop. There was that time at the shop. Mr Fuentes, the boss, said something about how someone had taken rum or whisky – someone had stolen from the shop.

Mr Fuentes called Saga, the other boy, and him.

'It's between both of you... I don't know what to say to you boys. You come to us for work. We give you work. And now you rob us. I don't know what to say to you boys.' Mr Fuentes was saying and looking from Saga to him, as if he expected to see the guilt spell itself out on their faces.

'I'm not sure which one of you is... the culprit. Or maybe it's both of you. I could hand you over to the police for this, you know, but I'm goin' to be generous with you. Tell me which of you took the goods and pay for them, or hand them back. Tell me and I won't worry with the police.'

The two of them, Saga and he, stood, not saying anything for a while; then Saga speaking, 'I di'n thief nutten, Mr Fuentes. I di'n thief nutten.'

Then Mr Fuentes looking fixedly at Saga for a while, then turning his eyes to Walter. 'You. What do you say?' And he said nothing; said nothing, just looked at Mr Fuentes.

'Well, well,' Mr Fuentes said, 'so you have nothing to say?'

He remained silent.

'I could fire both of you, you know. Could fire you or hand you over to the police, or both. You come asking for work, come begging for work, and this is what you return.' Mr Fuentes looking at Saga and speaking at Walter.

'No sense of gratitude, no sort of responsibility, no decency...'

And Saga saying, 'I didn't thief nutten, Mr Fuentes. I didn' thief nutten.'

'But I'll take it outa your pay. You bet. I'll take every cent of it. And any time anything like this happen again – out! Out you go!'

That time Walter exploded in a deep fury.

'Take Saga money if you want, Mr Fuentes. Take Saga money, but not mine. Not mine, because I didn't take nutten, and if you want, you could pay me off right now and let me go.'

Mr Fuentes, the fat Portuguese with the long thin nose, opened his big bloodshot eyes, and his face reddened. 'What!'

And Saga saying in between, 'I di'n thief nutten, Mr Fuentes. I di'n thief nutten, boss.'

'Well, for your damn freshness! For your freshness, I'll take every cent outa your pay and give you what's coming to you, and you can haul your thieving backside offa my premises right now.'

Mr Fuentes searching in his pocket – 'I'll give you what's coming to you' – and Walter flinging the bottle, not knowing how it came to be in his hands, not knowing what type of bottle it was, not spending time aiming, but flinging the bottle and seeing it connect on Mr Fuentes's chest, then ricochet into the partition and smash. Then he began to run, and even as he started, he saw Mr Fuentes holding his chest and shouting, 'Alec! Alec! Call the police! Quick! Call the police!'

And that time, running, running, panting and looking back; running until he came to the yard in which he lived, rushing through the door, bolting it and throwing himself on the bed. And sometimes in the night he used to jump up and listen to the darkness around him and wonder if the police were coming to get him; but all he heard that time was the thump of his heart trying to burst through his chest.

That time, and lying in the dark room, wondering and being afraid; wondering if Mr Fuentes had gone to the police; feeling sure that he had gone to the police, but hoping with a strong hope that he had not. Lying in bed during the daytime, reading a library book, and sometimes shutting the book – Shnap! – and thinking what a hell of a bitch-up place the world was, wondering why there had to be people like Mr Fuentes and why he had to have the misfortune to be bossed by them, wondering why his old man had whored and fought and drunk away thirty-five acres of good cocoa land that his father had left him, so that now he had to be catching hell, wondering who was responsible for all the pressure a man got, wondering who owned the world and who was paying to keep it the way it was, wondering what people were fighting for; wondering all that, and especially, when he would be able to stop running.

That time, and he had been running for three weeks; running

even when he was walking, even when he was sitting or sleeping; running and being afraid, until he met Saga one day. Met Saga up Siparia hill overlooking the Works and Hydraulics quarry yard, met Saga, and wanted to run; but he was going down and Saga was coming up the hill, and their eyes made four, and Saga started grinning.

'Wha' happening, man?' Saga said.

'Okay.'

'But you's a bitch, man,' Saga said. 'Suppose you'd hit the man on his head. You have a real bad temper. You's not a man to tie up with. Boy, a tess can't afford to get vex. A tess have to know how to live. You coulda buss the man head for nutten, and it woulda serve 'im right, but I wasn't looking for you to get in such a rage.'

'He went for police?'

'He was goin' for police. Was goin' for police an' then I tell 'im.'

'What yuh tell 'im?'

'Man, I didn't want to tell 'im, but when I think how he want to go for police an' how he want to get you lock up, an' when I think how I feel kinda glad to see how you connect 'im with the bottle (but you shoulda hit 'im in the solar plexus, he was bound to faint away) but you catch 'im a good shot in the chest an' I was glad to see the bitch hold 'is chest an' bawl out...'

'What you tell him?'

'Boy, in this world, a tess can't be stupid. A tess must be smart. 'Cause they smart, an' yuh have to be smart like them – smarter'n them – 'cause they have money an' brains an' all yuh have is yuh hands an' brains. So yuh have to be smarter'n them. But they mustn't know that. They must think yuh stupid. So I tell 'im how is I make contact with the bottl'a whisky. Yuh know, I just couldn't see yuh take the rap for something yuh didn't do, so I tell 'im is I make contact with the whisky, an' how yuh don't know a thing 'bout it, an' that must be why yuh get on yuh high horse when he say that yuh thief. Boy. An' how yuh know the bitch didn't want to call the police for the two of us? You for hittin' him with the bottle an' me for thiefing his whisky. But yuh see Alec! Alec is a good tess. Ol' greyhead Alec is a good tess, an' is he that beg Mr Fuentes not to send for the police. Alec talk yuh up, say how you's a quiet li'l fella don't get yuhself in nutten, an' how yuh's an honest tess. 'Cause the way Mr Fuentes lookin' was like he more vex as how yuh hit 'im than as how I thief 'im. Alec is a good tess. He used to quarrel with me, but is he who beg the boss not to send for the police, an' Mr Fuentes tell me to get offa his premises an'… an' that is that.'

'Well, I don't know what to tell you, Saga. Thanks, man.'

'Man, I was thinking how you's a fella wouldn't thief them. I can't understand why yuh wouldn't thief them, an' the pay done so small already; an' for me to come an' thief them and for you to go an' get stick-up in trouble was kinda hard. So I tell them… But yuh have to be smart. Yuh can't live stupid-stupid in this world. They have everything an' all yuh have is yuh brains an' yuh have to use 'em.'

'So he didn't call the police, eh?'

'Yuh have to thank Alec for that. Me too. Both o' we have to thank Alec for tossin' in a good word. But yuh sure let 'im have it. I don't know when yuh pick up the bottle. I only see it rocket offa his chest an' he bend over holdin' 'is chest an' that time the bottle done gone an' bounce off an' break in fine pieces on the wall. Yuh know, if the situation wasn't so damn critical I woulda laugh my belly full.'

'Well. I'm glad things turn out kinda all right.'

'Yuh musta been worried, eh? I could imagine how yuh was worried. Thinkin' how he send for police an' how police lookin' for yuh. Yuh was worried, eh?'

'Worried like hell.'

'Yuh's a good tess. But yuh have to be smarter'n that. Yuh have to be smart, 'cause that's all a tess can be – smart. They on top already an' yuh have to know that. Anyhow, I glad to see yuh to give yuh the talk.'

'I only sorry you lose your job.'

'That's life, man. A tess born to hussle. That's what it mean to be a tess – always husslin'.'

'Well, Saga, I going down.'

'Right, then. I goin' up by a calypsonian pardner here. I write a calypso an' Blakey say he goin' to see if he could get a break for me in the tent when it open. Well, I'll see yuh.'

'Okay, Saga.'

'Right, then.'

That time, going down the hill, he kept wondering why Saga had done such a thing for him when doing it could have landed him in deep trouble, and why greyhead Alec spoke out in favour of Saga and him. And he was thinking that Saga was a good tess, and greyhead Alec was a good tess too, although Alec used to get vexed sometimes and say how he didn't know what the younger generation was coming to. Yes, Alec was a good tess, because he wasn't bound to do what he did.

Then that time when he was assistant to a salesman on a van, going through the island, selling articles of clothing and other goods to the country folk that haggled and bargained in loud tones, and sometimes whispered in low vernacular that they couldn't afford to pay anything on their accounts that week.

That time, he had been about a year on the job and he knew most of the customers by name and what their men did for a living and how many children they had and what sort of jokes it was profitable to make with them.

It was evening and they were passing through Jerico, the village in which his mother lived, and he turned to the driver.

'Charles, drive up the next street, please. I want to see somebody up there.'

'Yuh know people up here?'

'Yes, man.'

'Well, I didn't know yuh know people up here.'

It was November and evening, and Charles swung the van around and went up the street on which his mother lived. There were about eight chickens in the street and Charles slowed down and allowed them to pass. They were small chickens and there was no hen with them, and afterwards, Charles exclaimed, 'Somebody goin' to eat chicken today!' and pointed to where a hen lay with its guts squashed out on the street, and the bloodstained motor car wheel-track around it.

There were many bumps and potholes along the road.

After a while, Charles said, 'Why the hell yuh bring me so far up here?'

'This ent far, man. It's just there.'

Charles laughed and he laughed too, because he remembered the calypso about how a fella was going to some part in the country and a girl told him, 'It ent far. Just there.' And how the place was really so far he never did get to it.

Charles drove slowly, and he saw the house: the unpainted house with the tall posts supporting it; one of the posts was leaning, and the pomerac tree in the yard was rich with purple blossoms, and at the side of the house the chaconia plant had leaves that were beginning to turn red, and there were weeds in the yard, and a giant governor banana tree with a heavy bunch reaching almost to the ground, and below the house was the frame of Boysie's old bicycle that had been there even before Pap got in the accident.

And sitting on the steps, the two children, clean and orderly, not like children at the home of their parents, but rather like children that had been sent to spend a day at a relative's and had been given careful and stern instructions not to behave like pigs, not to behave as if they had no training, but to keep themselves clean, to be quiet and not to run about and play in dirt or with the neighbours' dirty children, and the many such warnings given to children of poor inhibited folk when they are sent to a place where their parents believe that any spontaneous exercise of natural childish behaviour will bring shame upon their heads. They were sitting on the steps silently and very properly like a pair of caged animals that had exhausted every hope of escape and had resigned themselves to their fate.

And he, looking through the window of the vehicle, tried to smile, but his face felt stiff and he wondered what sort of appearance he presented to the children. Carol smiled, but Chris turned away without interest; then he saw one of them turn to face the house and he imagined, with sudden anxiety, that their mother – his mother – had called to them and was coming to the door.

'Go on, go on! Drive!' he said to Charles.

'I thought you wanted to stop here,' Charles said.

'No. You thought wrong. Drive!'

Charles drove up the street.

'What happen? Yuh forget who yuh goin' by?'

'No... I mean yes. Yes, man. I forget the exact house. Never see nutten so. Let's go back. Maybe another time.'

Charles turned the van around and they returned down the street, slowly.

'How long since yuh come up here?' Charles said.

'Must be about three years.'

'Whee-ee! Three years! A man could forget where his own mother livin' in three years.'

'Yeah.'

They drove down the street.

Charles said, 'Why yuh don't stop an' ask somebody if they know the people? They might help yuh. They could tell yuh if they move or what.'

'That's too much trouble.'

'Man, that ent no trouble. People in the world to help one another. I don't mind stoppin' a few minutes.'

'Is all right, Charles. Let's go on.'

'What happen? Yuh forget the name of the people?'

'No... Yes. I forget their name.'

'I don't know what to say to you young fellas. I don't know what yuh have to study to make yuh so forgetful. Yuh know, I's a man don't forget a name at all. Forget anything, but not a name since I know myself. Once, lemme tell yuh, once a Russian fella was workin' on the American base an' he had a long, complicate name that nobody could pronounce or remember. Sometimes a man just hear the name and he forget it. Not me. I never forget that name. Ask me now an' I'll tell yuh the name o' that tall white man, thin like a gaulin. Ferfichkin! Never forget that. You woulda forget that ages ago.'

'Some people have better memories than other, Charles.'

They passed the house again in going down. The children were no longer on the steps. He felt a great temptation to stop and go into the house and see his mother and his brother and sister.

Charles saw him looking at the house.

'This the house?' Charles asked.

'No,' he lied.

'Well, how yuh lookin' at it so?'

'A man can't look now?'

'All right,' Charles said. 'We better make it down to town.'

'Yeah. Gimme a cigarette, please, Charles.'

'Don't like to give my cigarettes to little boys. Bad habit.'

'Oh come on. Give a man a cigarette.'

'Ha, ha! Look who's man! Boy, when I was your age, I didn't leave my father house yet. Every day he had my backside on the land and sun used to be hotter than now. Every day. Dasheen, yam, cassava. And talk about hard land! That was hard land.'

'Gimme the cigarette, Charles.'

'Okay. But I don't like to give cigarettes to li'l fellas.'

That time, going down, Charles gave him the cigarette and he smoked in silence.

'How come yuh so quiet all on a sudden?' Charles asked.

'Sometimes a man don't feel to talk.'

'Thought you'd say yuh know people in the village?'

'Yeah.'

'Sure it wasn't that house with the pomerac tree and the two children in the yard by the steps?'

He didn't answer and Charles said seriously, 'Yuh shoulda stop off.'

Charles knew. How had Charles come to know? And all the way going down, he kept wondering how Charles had come to know, and kept thinking that perhaps he should have stopped off and visited with his folks.

Then it was a Sunday afternoon, three weeks after that time when he went up to Jerico with Charles driving the van and he had looked at the house but had not stopped to enter. That Sunday afternoon, he travelled to Jerico by taxi. The taxi dropped him at the end of the street and he walked for a quarter mile or more up the then deserted street until he came to the unpainted, wooden house with the high steps, and he looked once more at the scrubby yard and at the banana tree, and under the house, at the rusty bicycle-frame that belonged to his big brother Boysie.

That time, he carried some gifts for the family, and stood before the house clutching them as securely as a storeaway guards false papers, and his heart was beating fast and there was a weakness moving up past his knees to the pit of his stomach, and he couldn't say why that should be: whether it was because of fear or regret or through tenderness; he couldn't say why he felt so awkward. The wind blew that time, and bent the hedge and swayed the pomerac and banana trees, and at that moment he felt himself flooded by a soft tender feeling of longing; the intense longing of the prodigal and a love for his people, and he all but set out at a run through the yard and up the steps. But then the front door opened and his mother stood framed, frozen, in the doorway. With a frightening sense of dismay, he saw that she had not changed one bit in appearance: still the same inexpressive face, still the same quiet, careful woman: quiet and careful like the ugliest in the harem of a grouchy sultan – the same head, tied the same way, possibly with the same strip of cotton cloth. Three years and not a bit changed. Three years. Impossible! But there it was. There she was preserved in her unchange as something in deep-freeze, and at that moment he felt all the exuberance to greet her ooze from him like the juice from a pricked, overripe mango, and in its place an embarrassed, apologetic, apprehensive cloak fell upon him.

'Good evenin', Ma,' he said, starting to walk towards the door.

She stood there with no more curiosity than if he had come in from school; and with no more warmth, she said, 'Good evenin', Walter.'

He went up to her and kissed her on one cheek, and she stepped aside for him to pass inside.

In the house, Chris looked at him with interested eyes and Carol smiled shyly.

'You know who this is, Carol?' Walter said.

Carol looked at Chris.

'Walter,' Chris said.

'Walter,' Carol said, and smiled so her dimples showed plainly in her cheeks.

'Your brother,' the mother said, as if she were making an introduction.

He stood and looked at them: the two well-behaved children; and he felt a turning and twisting of his insides and he fell upon his knees and took hold of the two children, one in either hand,

and the parcels that he had brought with him fell to the floor and he didn't worry to pick them up.

He tickled Carol and she laughed, and he patted Chris on the back, and was quite absorbed in the children when he heard someone enter from the back door. He turned and saw it was Andrew. He was still on his knees that time.

'Well, big man, you come visiting,' Andrew said.

He raised himself to one knee and looked at his brother, and immediately he remembered the time when Andrew refused to go to Carmen's wedding although Pap had actually begged him to; and suddenly he became angry.

'Yes, I come visiting,' he said.

Andrew smiled thinly. Walter rose to his feet.

'You're a real big man,' Andrew said, looking at him, then chucking him playfully on the shoulder.

He made no reply. He didn't return the gesture. He stood looking at his brother.

'So you never come home eh, boy?' Andrew said, stepping backwards to have a good look at him.

No answer.

'So you went wild in town, I hear you even knock down a man with a bottle. Boy, I never expected to see you turn out like this.'

'Turn out like what?'

'Like this,' Andrew said. 'You leave your mother and family and now… Three years, eh! Three years, an' you now come back like the prodigal son in the Bible. All o' you the same; the same chip off the old block. Your father was a wild man an' you take after him. An' you had better schoolin' than the rest of us. An' look how you turn out. Where you workin'?'

He hesitated. 'I'm a salesman, kinda, on a van.'

'What happen to you, Walter? Why you don't get a decent little job? You went to high school. Not like me. Better you'd gone in the forest like Boysie. And still, Boysie had ambition. Boysie gone England. Where's your ambition, Walter? Only to make people shame. Don't know what get in your head to take up and leave home an' run away thinking you's man, to go on your own like an ownerless dog. Last time I see Ruth, she tell me how her husband aunt say sometimes you don't sleep in – a boy your age! You don't sleep in. Where you go when the night comes? Following bad company? You never even pass headquarters to look for me. Never even stop in to find out how Ma and the children making out. You gone all over town playing man, playing badjohn, pelting bottle to bring shame on your mother in her days. What happen? You don't care, or what? You don't care about nobody? You don't care about your own mother and family? Is all right if you don't care about me, but your own mother and family? They're all the people you have, and if you don't care about them, who you'll care about? What happen, Walter? You could get a nice little job if you try, but no! You don't think people care, you don't know people worried about what happening to you? Look at you? Wearing saga clothes. Is not to say you don't know better. Is not to say you didn't grow up in an all-right home. I don't know what to say. I don't know how you turn out so don't-care, and you had better chances than all of us. You went high school until you pick up yourself, thinking you's man and leave an' gone on your own. And now you come back with a few parcels and a smile, thinking you's the prodigal son and that somebody goin' to kill a fatted calf for you. We don't have no fatted calf to kill. I really don't know what to say…'

Walter cleared his throat to speak, but no words came that time. No words came.

Andrew speaking:

'You were goin' to school good-good, everybody saying, "Walter will come out something, Walter will be somebody in the family. Nobody was nutten, but Walter will be something, Walter will make the family raise its head. He will be an engineer or a lawyer or something, even a teacher…" You always like your book when you was small. But look at Walter now! Better you'd have no education. Better you'd gone and plough in the forest like the boys 'round here, and still, some of them have more ambition than you.

'Three years! And today is the first time your mother bless eyes on you, and you never see your brother Chris, or your little sister Carol. Stray like you have no ties, like you alone in the world.

'Sometimes I in town an' I hear a young fella get in trouble an' I wondering if is Walter get himself in something to make people

72

shame. While I trying to lift my head above water and to make the family something, you breaking down, you going about the town busting people head. Boysie gone England, Pap dead, and you gone wild. Well, well, well. I know you always had your own way. But not so.'

Walter listened, sure that Andrew would stop some time, either from hoarseness or through exhaustion; but Andrew continued.

'What you have in your pockets there? Cigarettes? A real big man! You never see Boysie smoke in this house and I sure you never see me smoke here, but you, the smallest, come in with a big pack of cigarettes like you's the only man in town. Your father say to Boysie and me, "Walter is the one with the brains. We better send him to high school," and Boysie and me agree; and when Boysie went England, is I pay your school fees. Boysie gone England and I sure you don't write him. When he write, he say, "What about Walter?" What about Walter? What I know about Walter? Can't see you. Don't know if you dead or alive or if you get yourself in trouble and the police pick you up and you in jail… But Boysie write from the cold of England, sending to ask "What about Walter? " And Mr Ramroop and Mrs Palmer and Mr Felix asking Ma about you. Your mother shame to say she don't know a thing about you… You're an intelligent boy, what you have to say?'

What could he say? He looked at Andrew.

Then his mother's voice broke in. 'You had lunch already, Walter?' She spoke in a choking voice, minus all emotion.

'Boy, your mother speaking to you,' Andrew said, quickly.

'I had lunch already,' he lied.

'I don't know what to say to you,' Andrew said. 'You didn't get such a bad start.'

'I'm not staying long, Ma.' He turned to his mother. 'Was just passing through.'

'That's it,' Andrew said hotly. 'He don't want nobody talk to him. He think he's too much man for somebody to talk to him.'

'Ma, I think I'm goin',' he said.

'All right, Walter,' his mother said. 'All right.'

'Chris, Carol, I'm goin', he said to the two little ones.

Andrew said nothing that time. He stood there looking as if he had been cheated.

And that time, leaving the house, he didn't look back because he wanted to prove to his brother and to himself that he was strong. He went down the steps, out through the yard and down the quiet Sunday street with the grass sprawling over the edges, with anger singing within him as it had sung that time when his father had died and his mother had waked him and had asked him to go quietly and call the neighbours and he had gone through the mist of his hot tears and the night and had called them despite the barking dogs and the hour.

And then, when it was nearing Christmas, how it was with the window shoppers looking in at the decorated windows, choosing their gifts without purchasing them, and how lonely he felt, and how he kept thinking of his loneliness, his thoughts going round and round as though they were fingers being dragged along the rim of a bicycle wheel – always returning to the same spot.

And when that Christmas came, he was lonely too. It was a cheerless, rainy day and he sat on the little cot in the little hut and listened to the beat of the rain on the roofing and the carols from the radio next door, and when the rain passed, he opened the one window of the room and saw groups of persons going by in bottle-and-spoon bands, singing snatches of calypsos and drinking rum, passing the bottle from hand to hand, drinking directly from the bottle, and when a steel-band passed beating '*Gloria in Excelsis Deo*', the loneliness heaped up in his heart and he lay down on the cot and began to cry, and Lester's aunt brought a basket with food and cake and a bottle of ginger beer for him and found him crying and he jumped up and wiped his tears hurriedly and told her thanks, and was ashamed that she had seen him crying; and then, eating the meal Lester's aunt had brought, his mind went back to the days before when he was at home and Pap was alive, how Pap used to sit at the head of the table and all the others used to be around and how they used to eat and drink and be merry on Christmas Day; and the tears came again to his eyes, and when he wiped them, they settled in his heart, and that time there was no way he could get rid of those tears.

And even when Christmas had gone, the tears were still in his heart and he felt that he knew then what it was to belong; and for all his leanings towards independence, he thought that he should return home, and he thought about Andrew and Ma and the unpainted house with the tall steps and he was afraid to go back home – or was it ashamed?

Then that time when he was coming back from Brothers Road, with Charles driving the van, he made up his mind.

They were going along the Tabaquite road, just after the Brasso police station, up that big hill with the spreading samaan trees and the beautiful tangle of vines and red hibiscus flowers on one side of the road and the green mountain on the other side, and down in the valley the immortelle flowering golden coins. That time, with the stillness of the road and its beauty and the birds sitting unafraid on the branches, he realized that he was very small indeed.

They were going up the hill, and Charles was a bit slow working the vehicle into second gear, and the van bucked and grumbled, and Charles said, 'Now Betsy. Don't play the arse. C'me on. Up the hill!' And the van grumbled and climbed up the hill from where you could see the sea in the far distance and the many shades of green vegetation spread between the sea and the hills.

'Charles.'

'Yes?'

'I think I want to leave the job.'

'When?'

'Right now.'

'Yuh want me stop the van an' put yuh out?'

'No, I mean this evenin'.'

'Well, say what yuh mean. Yuh get a new job?' Charles asked, not looking at him because a vehicle was coming down and Charles was looking straight at the road.

'No.'

'Well, what happen? Yuh win a sweep?'

'No.'

'Yuh serious?'

'Yes, man.'

'Yuh want to leave? Yuh not gettin' enough money? Nobody gettin' enough money these days… If yuh not getting enough, ask the boss for a raise. He might give yuh. Yuh's an all-right fella an' I'll put in a word for yuh. But yuh'll have to ask the boss yuhself. The last boy was workin' with me wasn't gettin' enough money an' is I tell him to ask for a raise. That's how yuh gettin' what yuh gettin' now. But that boy was no damn good. Like to cuss an' play mannish – yuh know what I mean?'

'Well, I leavin' the job.'

'I mean, just like that – for no reason?'

'Sure, I have a reason.'

'Well, I hope yuh know what yuh doin'. I always advise a man when yuh leavin' a job, yuh must know where yuh stretchin' yuh hand when Friday evenin' come… If yuh know that, well, okay. But a boy like you shouldn't see too much trouble. Yuh have brains an' yuh not rude – only a little temper. Well, nobody's perfect. A man must have a fault. Take me: I don't like to comb my hair. I mean, I still does comb it, but I don't like the idea… Well, Mr Poon goin' to have to find a man to replace yuh. I alone not makin' these runs. If he want me to do the wuck alone, he have to come up with more cash, and even so, I still can't imagine me alone doin' all this wuck – drivin' an' sellin' an' arguin' with people an' keepin' book. I don't know where he goin' to get somebody to put in your place. See the last boy was wuckin' with me the other day, Stanley, say he wanta wuck. I tell him: "Boy, yuh don't want wuck. Yuh want to be a sagaboy an' that outa season." I done tell Mr Poon if that boy wuckin' with me, I done wuck. He too damn rude an' careless… Well, Mr Poon goin' to have to get a new man to put in yuh place. I alone not makin' these runs.'

'Charles, you think things could just keep on goin' bad in a man's life all the time… without change?'

'Boy, I see people ketchin' hell from mornin'.'

'And no change?'

'Sure, sure, change from bad to more worst. But you young. Yuh'll get thru. All yuh have to do is to be decent an' respectable so people will like yuh an' give yuh a little push. Plenty fellas get through so – decent, respectable boys with no Cambridge Cer- tificate, an' they get good-good jobs with government and some with private companies. When the boss say something, they agree even if they don't like the idea, an' the boss get to like them.'

'I don't know if I could do that.'

'Yes, you could do it. Good boys get good-good jobs easy so.'

'I don't know if I could do that.'

'Boy, a man don't know what he could do. But yuh didn't tell me where yuh leavin' the job to go.'

'Goin' back home.'

'Home? That's a good place to go, but – '

'But what?'

'But yuh have to know how yuh goin'.'

'What you mean?'

'I mean that sometimes a man does think: Well, I goin' home an' Ma will cook me food an' Ma will wash me clothes an' everything will be good… But, I guess that depends on the family. Yuh know what I mean?'

'I understand… Charles, I hope you don't think I'm a bitch how is only now I tell you I – '

'That's all right, man. I mean, is true you didn't tell me, but you had yuh reasons. An' anyway that ain't nutten.'

'You see, Charles, I was thinking about it all the time and then today, coming up the big hill just after the police station, I decided. Anyhow, I don't know if I'll change my mind when we reach in the yard.'

'Mr Poon goin' to have to get a man to replace yuh. I hope he get a sensible boy. Stanley wasn't so stupid, but that boy was rude. I goin' to have to tell Mr Poon that I alone can't make these runs.'

And then they reached down in the yard and he told Mr Poon and he paid him off, and he had two dollars that he owed Charles and he gave it to Charles.

'Well, Charles, I'm goin'.'

'Well, boy, I hope yuh know what yuh doin'. I hope yuh get through. Just act decent. Plenty young fellas who didn't have no Cambridge Certificate get through so. The boss will like yuh an' yuh'll be surprised to see how far yuh'll reach with a smile an' yuh mouth shut.'

'Okay, Charles. I hope you get a good fella to work with you.'

Then that time he went to the place where he stayed and he

gave Lester's aunt the rent he owed her, and told her that he was going back home. She said that she was glad and that she was sorry and that he should pass around to see her any time he was in Port of Spain, and that he wasn't to forget to tell his mother how-de-do for her. He went to the room and packed up his belongings, then he left, intending to go home to Jerico.

Then, when he was at the corner of Prince and Henry Streets, waiting for a taxi to take him to Jerico, he saw Andrew stepping across from the direction of the Red House, stepping with correct military strides and looking at him from under the peak of his cap. He stood and waited for Andrew to come up.

'Good evenin', Andrew.'

'Good evenin', Walter. Like yuh travellin'?'

'Yes, I'm goin' home.'

'Home? How long yuh stayin' this time? Last time I try to give you a little advice and you get so damn vex, you walk out the house. How long you staying this time?'

'I'm goin' back home for good.'

'You mean you goin' home to stay? What happen? You get into some kinda trouble?'

'I didn't get in no trouble.'

'I can't understand. You sure you not in any trouble?'

'Yes, Andrew. I'm sure.'

'Well, you know you'll have to behave yourself, Walter?'

'Why you tellin' me that, Andrew?'

'Because... because I know you, boy. Three years you turn your face from your family. You didn't care what happen to them. Else you wouldn't pelt bottle at people and look for trouble to bring shame on your mother head, and – How many times you went home? How many times?'

'Once.'

'Three years! And you went home once. You call that behavin'?'

'I'm not arguing, Andrew. I don't want to argue.'

'You feel you's too much man. Don't want nobody to talk to you. What you goin' home for? Ma seeing enough trouble with those two at home, so you better behave yourself.'

'I don't understand why you getting on so, Andrew.'

'I don't care what you don't understand.'

'This is a hell of a world, and you's a hell of a brother.'

'What you mean?'

'Just that.'

'I don't understand you, Walter.'

'You... you'll never understand me, Andrew.'

'Don't give me no rudeness in the street, you hear. Where you goin'?'

'Up the road.'

'You not goin' home? I thought you said you goin' home.'

'Home! What you call home?'

'Walter!'

'You go to hell, Andrew.'

'Boy!'

'You go to hell, Andrew,' he cried and took off up the street, as fast as anger could carry him.

3

'You're so quiet,' the woman says. 'I thought you were asleep.'

'I'm not asleep,' the man says, straightening himself in the chair and groping to establish connection with the present.

'So I see. You were so quiet.'

'I was thinking,' he says, opening his eyes and becoming aware of the Sunday morning in the living-room of the apartment on the third floor of the tenement building on Webber Street, and of his wife standing next to him. 'I was thinking,' he repeats.

'Oh! I really thought you were asleep.' She is standing quite close to him, her rump actually touching his knees.

'Carol come back yet?' he asks.

'Yes.' She sits on the arm of the chair. 'But she forgot to bring the morning paper. She's gone for it. You know girls.'

She presses her body roguishly against his, then slides from the arm of the chair into his lap. Usually that meant that he would kiss her on the neck; she would draw away and he would reach for her with his arms – he often thought that her object was to see exactly how far his arms could stretch – then she would charge into his arms, almost toppling him. He had grown wise with experience: when he kissed her now, if she drew away he allowed her to. Gradually, the reaching and the rushing and the almost toppling over had subsided. So this time he doesn't kiss her, and she leans backwards and brushes her head against his forehead. He resists the temptation.

'You're tired?' she asks.

'Yes, I'm tired. I want to see the papers before I take a rest. Carol's printing the papers, or what?'

'You know Carol. She doesn't walk, she strolls. Your sister should've been a princess.'

'And she could've been if…'

'If…?'

'If the old man hadn't been such a fool. If he hadn't fêted and frigged his lands away.'

'Oh, hush about that, Walter.'

'You asked,' the man says.

They are silent for a few moments. The wife gets off the husband's lap and goes and takes a chair.

'You think it'll be a boy?' she asks.

'What?'

'The baby.'

'Yes,' he says tiredly.

'Why you think it'll be a boy?'

'Because you want me to think so. People are happy when you think as they want you to. But that wouldn't make it a boy.'

There is another stretch of silence.

'Cherrie won't be so lonely now,' the woman says. 'The psychologists say it's bad to be an only child.'

'They can say anything. They don't have to mind them.'

'But, darling, the economists say that it's almost as expensive to keep one as it is to keep two.'

'Yeah. My arithmetic tells me one and one make two.'

'Why you snapping at me?'

'I'm not snapping at you. Look! If you don't want me to snap, why don't you say something sensible?'

'You're edgy this morning.'

'Yes.'

'I forgive you, Walter.'

'Thanks, Stephanie.'

'You going to repaint the living-room for Christmas?'

'I don't know.'

'I thought you said you'd repaint it.'

'What's the matter with you?'

'I only asked if you're going to repaint the living-room. You said you'd repaint it… I only asked.'

'Well, for Christsake, Stephanie! If I said I'd do the thing, I'll do it.' He gets off the chair swiftly as if his action is a part of what he wants to say. 'What's wrong with me this morning? What's wrong?'

'You're…'

'All right, all right. Don't tell me, doctor. Don't.' He resumes his seat. 'I know I'm nervous and edgy.'

'I wasn't going to say that. And I never said you were nervous and edgy. I wish I could do something to please you.'

'Why don't you tell me a story and put me to bed?'

'All I want is a home and children and you,' the wife says, close to tears.

'And you have none of them. This nasty little joint is no home; you have only one child; and me… of course, you have me,' the man says, his voice scratching like wind-blown dried leaves on a pitched walk.

'No.' Her voice is thin. He knows the sign. She has become the half-infant, half-woman. 'I have none of them. Only when you're not in these moods, when you're not thinking about fighting governments and people… Sometimes when you're tired from working and we go to bed, and sometimes when you've had a few drinks and come home giggling and puke down the place and I have to take off your socks and wash your face and clean up the mess, and other times, other times when…'

'When I tumble into bed with you?' He makes it sound obscene – pig's dung on the dried, wind-blown leaves.

'Not even those times. Not those times. I mean, when you're not so huge and strong and untouchable. When you feel beaten and you want my breasts to pillow your head; those times I feel I have a husband. But you'll never change the world, Walter. You'll never scratch the world.' She sighs deeply and the tears leak into her voice. 'You ask me to tell you a story and put you to bed, well, I don't know any story to tell. All I want is a home and children, but God alone knows what you want… What you want, Walter?'

'I just want to be a man,' he says. 'I just want to know and to feel that I'm a man.'

'You're a man,' his wife says.

'By your say-so?'

'I try to make you feel happy. I try,' she says, the tears trembling in her voice and beginning to flow from her eyes. She makes no effort to stem the flow. It is as if she wants him to see exactly how human and tender she is.

'There are some things which a man must hold on to, Stephanie,' the man says, with no apology in his tone.

'I wonder what's the use of those things.'

'I wonder too,' the man answers. 'I wonder what would happen if I cut out my balls. But I don't cut them out because I wonder.'

'If I could understand,' the woman says, 'what you're fighting, maybe I could help. You can't blame me for being just a normal woman, with normal desires.'

'Who's blaming you?'

'You can't blame me for not seeing the things, the shadows, you're struggling with.'

'They're not shadows.'

'To you they're not, but to me. I have no idea what most of it is all about.'

'Do you try? Do you try to understand?'

'You know I try. But all I see is people coming into the world and trying to make their positions better, trying to secure a few comforts. I see people in this very city, doing all kinds of jobs just to improve their positions. I don't see people giving up and running off to the country.'

'So you see people trying to improve their positions?' the man says.

'Yes. If you don't have, you don't count, and all of us want to count, to be something, to have something.'

'No matter how it comes; we just want to count.'

'I'm not saying that, Walter. But everybody know they have to fight for what they want. Nobody gives anybody anything or does anything for anybody... But I don't know what you want.'

'I've told you. I want to be a man with two balls.'

'How you going to be that man, Walter? How? By running to the country on a piece of hard land with a hoe and a dirty sleeveless merino from mornin' 'till night; by running away from bosses and people; by leaving the world? Oh Jesus, Walter. You can't do that.'

'Why don't you shut up?' he says, and leans back in the chair.

'Walter!'

'I... Sorry... I didn't mean that. It's just – '

'Life is so short,' the woman says. 'All this struggling and – so short.'

'Yes. And a man is alone.'

'You're not alone, Walter.'

'I've always been alone. I know that now.'

'You shouldn't say that.'

'It's true. That's one thing marrying you didn't change.'

'Lord! You are cruel.'

'And truthful.'

'Why you married me, then?'

'I don't know,' he says, straightening up in the chair and looking at her. 'I guess I was in love with you. Anyway, I didn't enquire about your disposition to living in the country.'

'You needn't sound so bitter,' the woman says.

'Do I sound bitter?'

'Look, darling, let's not argue again.'

'Leave me alone, then,'

'All right. Okay, sir.' She gets off the chair, turns and leaves the room, looking back, as if she expects him to follow. He does not follow. He sinks backwards into the chair. And again his mind goes back to days past.

4

And now Walter thinks of that time after he had left Andrew staring open-mouthed at him and he walked away up Henry Street with his grip in his hand and anger beating against his temples.

He walked hurriedly, as if he knew where he was going, and when he reached to Park Street and stood waiting for the flow of traffic to subside before he crossed the street, up came Saga with a big grin splitting his shiny black face.

'Well, well,' Saga said. 'You's just the man I want to see. What happenin'? Who vex you?'

And he tried to grin, and shook Saga's hand, but didn't tell him of the incident just past with his brother; and Saga said again, 'Man, I want to see you bad.'

'For what?'

'Let's go drink a beer and I'll tell yuh.'

And Saga led the way and he walked behind, holding the big grip carefully so as to avoid bouncing the legs of other pedestrians. When they reached the beer shop, Saga called for two beers and they began to drink.

'Yes, man,' Saga said. 'I in a big jam. I was lookin' for yuh. A man have to know his tesses. Yuh have to know who is a shit-up tess, who is a bluff tess and who is a good tess. You's a good tess.'

'What's the jam?'

'Is about a girl. A nice girl. Nicest girl I ever had. Decentest girl. A real nice social girl from Woodbrook, an' all the tesses say how I's a lucky man to get such a nice girl. So I want to write her a letter – you know, she gone Tobago for a month and I want to write her 'cause she write me, and I really write a letter, but some of the spellin' an' things not so right though the letter have some big words in it. Yuh know what I mean, when yuh writing to a real social nurse-girl yuh have to write good, an' you's a man who went to high school an' yuh not ignorant, so yuh must know some big words an' some grammar to lash out with, 'cause is only one real big word I know – philoprogenitiveness – hardly any others. Acknowledged not so big, eh?'

And he had wanted to laugh a good hearty laugh that time when he heard that that was the sort of jam Saga had found himself in.

'What does philopro-whatever-it-is mean?'

'Philoprogenitiveness, an' not one of the tesses could spell it, much more to tell the meaning. I drop the word on a stupid civil servant girl who livin' in the lane near by me and she didn't know it mean love of youth, an' yet, she's one girl use to play social for me.' Saga pushed his hand in a pocket. It came out with an envelope.

'I draft up a letter here and I had was to post it before she come back, but lucky for me I see yuh now, so yuh could correct what I have and even splice in a few big words an' some real grammar to suit a nice social girl.'

Walter took the envelope from Saga and opened it. He read:

My darling Evangeline, yore beautie is beyond compare in my philoprogenitiveness I seek now to make you acknowledged of the deepness of my emoshun for you which is beyond me to express. There is no other one in my life or in my days or in my nights who I feel such affeckshun for as you that afflick me with such deep and tender passhon so deep and loving when I think of you or sound your sweet name on my thick lips like honey.

Of course you know I feel this deep and burnin desire and tender moment in my life for you more than anyone in my life from since that night when we dance the bolero and I hold you so gintle friken that you break in my strong arms my love divine.

Since that night I cannot sleep one wink without thinkin of your face or eyes situate like two marbles I had when I was a little boy and could pitch and win everybody in Nelson street.

And how I make myself acknowledged of you of the real deep and tender passhon in my heart for you are the one I love.

There is a dance at Sea Farers a social place and it will be a social fete with social people and not scamps when you come down from your true holiday you are spending in the beautiful islan I will be longing to see you always and I will like to take you to the theatre on Sunday when you come because you say you coming on Wednesday after next. A nice picture with Alan Lad is showin if you can come. I will be happy happy.

I remain,

your ever true and loving boy,
Winston called Saga

When Walter lifted his eyes from the letter, Saga said, 'Yuh see, when yuh writin' these social folks yuh have to impress them to make them respect yuh. So I want yuh to help me. I had a book I used to take out words from and I lend it to a tess to write a letter an' how yuh know the thiefing scamp never remember the address. The big words must catch she and right away she'll know she not dealin' with one o' those ignorant tesses who can't spell they own name.'

'I didn't know your name was Winston.'

'So many tesses don't know that. Everybody call me Saga. An' if I tell yuh my real name, yuh bawl.'

'What?'

'Winston Clunis Wiltshire! Beat that! So yuh'll help me with the letter?'

'Sure.'

'Well, what about wuck? Yuh wuckin'?'

'I was working but I left the job to go home by my mother.'

'An' what happen? Yuh not goin' again?'

'No.'

'Boy, wish I had a mother to go by... Yuh know, for carnival I did a little singing in the calypso tent. If I'd see yuh, yuh woulda get a free ticket to come an' hear me. So yuh not wuckin'. I not wuckin' either. Tomorrow I want to go up to a place called Nuggle. My cousin have a place up there an' sometimes I go up there to spend time an' do a little hard wuck when I want. Wait! Yuh say yuh not wuckin'?'

'Yes, I left the job yesterday; but I think I could get it back if I go tomorrow.'

'Why yuh don't let's go up Nuggle?' Saga said. 'Good tesses up there. We does cook an' hunt an' things an' I'll write a couple calypso an' yuh don't have to have money. Let's go. Take a holiday from the town an' the husslin'. Too many husslers down here.'

'I don't know,' Walter had said, thinking quickly.

'Lissen man!' Saga said. 'Yuh married? No. Yuh wuckin'? No. Well, let's go. Nothing to keep yuh in town.'

'I better give this town a rest,' Walter said, thinking.

'Yes,' Saga agreed, 'give the blasted town a rest. Yuh don't know what the country will bring.'

'Okay, I'll go. But I don't know how long I'll stay.'

'Man,' Saga said. 'When yuh reach up there yuh wouldn't want to leave.'

'All right,' Walter said. 'And I'll write the letter tomorrow.'

'What about this evening?'

'I can do it, but you'll have to come up by where I used to stay.'

'Well, let's go,' Saga said.

And he went by the place where he stayed before he gave up the key because he was leaving to go to Jerico, up by his mother. And Lester's aunt allowed him to remain there that night; and he wrote the letter for Saga, and on the following day, left with Saga for Nuggle.

Saga and he reached Nuggle about half past two in the afternoon. When they arrived, the streets were deserted and the crude wooden houses covered with carrat leaves stood off the road like some terrible brown animals that had invaded the village and had either swallowed the human inhabitants or had chased them off to the forest that stood tall and silent on all sides.

'Saga, where's everybody?' he asked.

'Gone to work,' Saga told him.

'The children?'

'Gone to school.'

'All of them?'

'The others inside.'

'What about the women?'

'Most of them gone to work in the forest, but the others inside sleeping.'

'This place looks real dead to me. Even the shop close.'

'Wait till four o'clock when children start coming from school and the trucks start bringing people from the forest.'

'All right.'

'Don't be afraid. The action begin at four. Let's go up by my cousin.'

They went up by where Clayto, Saga's cousin, lived. Clayto wasn't home, but the door was unlocked and they went in and unpacked and looked about for something to eat. There was some flour and a piece of salt-fish. Saga made a bake from the flour and roasted the piece of salt-fish and they ate and left piece of the bake and piece of the roasted salt-fish for Clayto. Just before four o'clock they went down the road by the junction.

They were just in time to see the shop opening and the first band of school children going home. Then the main body of school children came down the streets, hopping and skipping and waking the village with their noises, and doors began to be thrown open, heads of women to emerge, and the shrill voices of women to be raised in reprimand of the unruly. Then, in the midst of all that, the first truck arrived with logs and with men, women and dogs perched atop the logs. The men got down first, then pulled their dogs down, then lifted their tools down, then helped the women down. And there was loud talking and laughing and joke-cracking; and it was as if the villagers had returned from an excursion to the beach instead of from a hard day's labour in the forest.

Long afterwards, even when darkness had fallen, trucks were pulling up at the junction, and lines of dusty, sweaty workers with tools on their shoulders and dogs at their heels were arriving on foot.

Clayto, Saga's cousin, arrived on the very last truck, and Saga, who was sitting on the culvert talking to some fellows, didn't recognize him until he reached right up to him.

Afterwards Saga introduced Clayto to Walter, and the three of them walked over to the house. Clayto was glad that they had come because he had some important work and was pressed for time. He hoped they would help him.

That night they remained a long time talking about Port of Spain: of the places one could visit and of the beautiful women stepping down Frederick Street on a Friday afternoon, and of the women Clayto had been friendly with the time he had lived at St James. After that, they went to bed because they had to rise early to go to help Clayto cross-cut logs in the forest.

On the following day Clayto waked them while the morning was still grey and misty and on all sides farm cocks were heralding the rising sun. They prepared a meal, part of which was breakfast and part to be used for lunch, then they went down by the junction to wait on the first truck. And when the truck came they boarded it along with the men, women and dogs that had been awaiting its arrival. On the road they passed men and women walking. The first group signalled the truck to a stop and got aboard, but the truck did not stop for the others because by then it was already full. Those aboard the truck laughed heartily at those that were walking, and called out crude jokes to them while they were within hearing.

The truck rattled on until Clayto reached that part of the forest where he was working. He banged on the bonnet of the truck, and other persons on the truck joined in the banging until the driver stopped the vehicle and those working in that area got down.

That day Saga and he cross-cut logs while Clayto drove the tractor, and in the evening they came down tired and went by the standpipe to wash themselves.

Saga was always on the lookout for the water patrol, because the last time he had been at Nuggle one of the patrol men had caught him bathing at the standpipe and was going to arrest him because it was against the law, and Saga had cuffed the man and slipped away from his grasp; so Saga was always on the lookout for the water patrol, especially for the man he had cuffed and run away from. The fellows knew that. It gave them the opportunity to play a regular joke on Saga.

Any time Saga was bathing, they would shout, 'Saga! Look, the water police!' And before they could finish uttering p-o-l-i-c-e, Saga would be yards up the street, and when he looked back there would be, not the water patrol, but a group of laughing young men. Sometimes Saga cursed them for their pains, but often he laughed and told them that if they kept him in training that way, when the patrol did come they would never be able to catch him.

That week they worked with Clayto, cross-cutting logs and sometimes helping him man the trailer of the tractor he was driving, but on Saturday they didn't go to work. Nobody worked on Saturday, except in an emergency, or unless he happened to be a charcoal-burner with a charcoal pit afire. Saturday was payday.

That Saturday, they slept late into the morning, and after they had prepared breakfast, went down by the junction where they met other villagers waiting for pay. And afterwards, those contractors who had purchased wood during the week came in cars and paid the subcontractors, who in turn paid their workmen. Then the fête began.

Clayto paid Saga and Walter for the work they had done during the week, and they all went in the rum shop and Clayto bought a bottle and called some of his friends, and they all stood there in the rum shop and drank; and after a while, Saga, who wasn't as fond of rum as he was of gambling, gave Walter the eye and they left the company and went under the old house by Mack, where the fellows were playing whappie. They remained there for the entire evening and left only when night had fallen. That first Saturday he won a few dollars and Saga and he went home whistling a calypso in the dark.

Two years he spent at Nuggle, and he learned to play whappie and to roll dice and to drink rum, and he came to know about the place and about the people and the pattern their lives took. And it was a sort of education, looking on with a sort of detachment, watching the folks and listening and understanding. It was only afterwards when wood was becoming scarce that work began to fall off and fellows began to remain idle at the junction; before that, everyone worked hard and prayed for Saturday.

There were two sets – the drinkers and the gamblers; and there was one set that both drank and gambled. On Saturdays the drinkers remained in the rum shop until it closed, or sat under the mango tree near the culvert and talked and drank. When a bottle was consumed, if the shop was closed, they would go and beat on the galvanized iron fence near the window, and Chin himself or his wife Betty would sell to them through the window. On Sunday mornings it was the accepted practice to purchase at the window and to drink under the mango tree near the culvert. Only the more successful subcontractors and the sergeant and the Forest Rangers drank their whisky or rum down in the back of Chin's shop.

The gamblers went under the old house by Mack as soon as they had been paid, and left after they had won, or – usually – lost. When one of the younger fellows won, he would take some friends with him and they would go down to Port of Spain and look for whores to make 'fares' with on George Street or in a cheap nightclub. They returned early Sunday morning, sat on the culvert, and waited for the tesses coming to start the Sunday-morning whappie, to tell them what a good time they had had.

There was gambling all day Sunday. There was whappie and four-hand rummy and single-hand rummy and dice.

Sunday night the villagers went to bed, and Monday morning they rose early and went to the forest by truck or on foot and they would work the entire week until Saturday, when they would wait on the contractors to come up and pay the subcontractors who would pay them. Sometimes the contractors came up early and the fête began early; and sometimes, according to arrangement, the subcontractors went down and met the contractors, then returned to pay the workmen; and sometimes the workmen remained waiting for the contractors or subcontractors for the whole day. And you heard them asking: 'Yuh see Mr Dass? Yuh see Carerra?' No. You hadn't seen Mr Dass. No. You don't know where Carrera is. And they would shrug and go and sit unhappily on the culvert and wait.

So many Saturdays he spent under the old house by Mack, gambling. Everybody gambled. No one asked why. No one asked, Why do I gamble? Why don't I save my money and buy a power-saw, or build a concrete house with high steps and good galvanized iron roof, and fence it round with chicken-wire and plant some anthuriums in the front and grow some lettuce and tomatoes in the back…? Everybody gambled.

So much had happened there under the old house by Mack.

There was that time Varney had sold two Berkshire pigs and a crop of dry corn. Varney had been a charcoal-burner, but he had stopped working in the forest, had taken a woman, and together they had cultivated a piece of land and had reared some chickens and some pigs. That Saturday evening he sold the pigs and corn and came down by the shop to collect the money from the man that had made the purchase. He intended to go to Port of Spain on Monday morning to pay the first instalment on a second-hand van, so he didn't even take a drink. No one knew why he came under the old house by Mack before he went home. He came under the old house there and he felt so big and tall that he almost bounced his head on one of the sills below the house. The tesses were playing whappie that time and one of them, seeing him, said: 'Yes. Look! A good-tess reach.' And someone moved around and gave Varney a seat.

It was a hot evening. The gamblers were sweating and some of them carried no handkerchiefs to wipe their faces, so the sweat ran down their cheeks. Some allowed it to drip and fall on the ground and some wiped it away with their bare palms.

Varney sat under the old house with his money in his pocket and a smile on his face, and he lost the smile and he lost his money, and the Casa gave him two dollars and he bet that and lost it also.

That time it was very quiet under the old house and Varney rose to a stooping position and all eyes were on him, expecting some sort of action; and Varney squatted there with the smell of pigs about him and sweat breaking out like a rash on his forehead and running zig-zag down his cheeks; and he took a handkerchief from his pocket and held it close to his face and then put it back in his pocket without making use of it; and somebody said, quietly, like he was sorry: 'Varney, yuh forget to wipe yuh face.' And Varney took out the handkerchief again and wiped his face. It was a brown handkerchief and it cost twenty-eight cents by Chin, and sold for eighteen cents apiece on Charlotte Street, Port of Spain. Varney wiped his face and the veins stood out like rope on his neck and like cord on his forehead, and the tesses were looking at him, expecting him to do something drastic, but all he did was to turn over the top card on the pack. It was Jack of Spades, and he rested it face upwards alongside the rest of the pack and kept gazing at it.

Night was falling that time and one of the tesses lighted the flambeau. That same time, a fellow from the street shouted: 'Varney! Varney!' And Varney squatted with his knees drawn up under his chin and wouldn't answer. The fellow poked his head under the old house, and seeing Varney's position, called in a different tone: 'Varney?' And Varney turned his head slowly and looked at him, and his back was soaking with sweat.

'Varney, yuh little boy out in the road lookin' for yuh,' the fellow said.

'That's all?' Varney asked.

The fellow nodded, yes.

'Tell him to go home.'

And that time Varney didn't have a cent to make medicine with. And someone asked, 'Who playing four-hand rummy?' But no one was playing. The winners had left. Varney swallowed some saliva, cleared his throat, dusted his seat, and crawled out from under the old house.

And afterwards, just after Varney had gone and the tesses could draw their breaths, Charleau said, 'This is a hell of a world.' And the tesses looked at him like they were listening with their eyes, because they knew Charleau was about to begin a discussion.

'Losers and winners. What's the difference?' Charleau said. 'What's winnin' an' what's losin'?' Charleau had one ear. He said one night some dogs cornered him in a garage at Arima; he strangled one, but one bit off an ear. Now he threw out his words challengingly, pushed back his cap on his head and waited for comment.

Dougla cleared his throat. He always cleared his throat before speaking. He said it was a smoker's cough.

'Hem-hem. Don't be an arse, Charleau. Winnin's winnin' an' losin's losin'.'

'Think so?' Charleau said.

'Yes. Hem-hem. Winnin's winnin' an' losin's losin'. Yuh win

a dollar, yuh lose a dollar: one is gain, one is loss. I think yuh makin' yuhself an arse, Charleau.'

'All right,' Charleau said, 'but I want to say it don't have winners in the world.'

'Yuh makin' yuhself more arse now, Charleau,' Dougla said. 'It must have winners an' losers.'

'Why?'

'It must.'

'Nothing must.'

'Hem-hem, Charleau, when a man lose money, what is that? Lose. When a man win money, what is that? Win.'

'Yuh soundin' good, Dougla, but I still say it don't have winners.'

'It – hem-hem – bound to have winners if it have losers.'

'An' if yuh think I lie,' Charleau said, 'I could bring the book I read it outa an' show yuh.'

'Yuh always talkin' 'bout some book,' Jarroo said.

'Jarroo, you hush yuh arse. If yuh see yuh own name big like the Red House yuh wouldn't know is yours. You hush.'

'Yuh just showin' off 'cause yuh does read one or two book,' Jarroo said.

'Shut up, Jarroo. Shut up, let the people talk,' Dolphus said.

Dougla said, 'A man must win an' a man must lose. Don't tell me is only losin'. Yuh see any sense in that?'

'Ah-ha,' Charleau said. 'Yuh hit my point. It doesn't have to make sense. Lemme ask yuh something.'

'Ask,' Dougla said.

'A man does live an' fight to live an' he must dead. Yuh see any sense in that?'

'That different,' Dougla said.

'Different, my eye. A man must dead. Yuh see any sense in that?'

'No.'

'No. Yuh can't see any sense in that because it ent have no sense in that. That is just how it is.' Charleau's tone was full with triumph.

'If yuh know a man can't win,' Dougla said, 'why yuh gamble, then?'

'Gamblin' is life. Because I bound to dead, I don't have to stop my life. Gamblin' is life. Win or lose, yuh bound to play.'

The following afternoon Reynold got himself in big trouble.

It was Sunday and a few tesses were coasting on some old-talk while Reynold, a slim, quiet fellow, was playing single-hand rummy with Shovel, a talkative, big-chested fellow who worked on a truck loading gravel and boulders from Arena and sometimes from Claxton Bay and Biche. The tesses coasting on the old-talk didn't see what happened, they only heard Shovel bawl out and Reynold scream, and when they looked around they saw Shovel on the ground with the side of his head bashed in and the piece of iron with the blood on it on the ground right there next to Shovel. The tesses lifted Shovel. He was a heavy fellow, and Reynold helped them carry him to the roadside and they stopped a taxi and put him in and two of them went with him to the hospital in Sangre Grande.

'What happen? What happen?' everybody wanted to know; and Reynold, through his tears, said: 'He dead! He dead! He thief me. He thief me. He do it twice an' was goin' to do it again just because he bigger'n me an' everybody 'fraid him. He thief me an' he was goin' to do it again just because he bigger'n me.'

The police came in a jeep and took the iron with the blood on it. It was a long iron peg on which Martin tied his goat. The police took it and they took Reynold and carried him up Sangre Grande.

'How much they was playin' for?'

'A penny a pot.'

'A penny a pot!'

And they carried Reynold to Sangre Grande and there was nobody to stand his bail, and when the case was called, they gave him three years in jail, and after he came from hospital, Shovel was paralysed all down his right side.

'Gamblin'! See what happens in gamblin',' the villagers said. 'They will kill a man for a penny in a gamble.'

And after that the police jeep used to pass around regularly to see if the tesses were gambling under the old house, but the tesses moved fast whenever they heard the police approaching and the police never caught anyone except Dolphus, when he remained behind one time to grab the money the others had left on the ground when they ran. The police caught Dolphus with his fists full with money and they asked no questions; a policeman dropped the rawhide on his back and he shouted, 'Fire! Fire! Out the fire!' And when the other lash fell across his shoulders, he fell on his knees and began to recite the rosary. They took the money from him and set him loose and he ran up the street at full speed as if they were behind him.

'What happen?' the tesses asked Dolphus.

'Fire,' Dolphus said. 'They have a fire down there.' And after that they called Dolphus Fire-Down-There.

Yes, there was plenty action under the old house by Mack.

And on the culvert there was talk. On weekday evenings after work. Tesses used to go and sit on the culvert, for hours, just to talk and crack jokes. There was so much to hear.

One night Uncle Bogo, barefooted, but dressed in an old jacket with a handkerchief tied about his neck, stopped at the culvert to ask the tesses if Ma Florence, who had been a long time ailing, had died. When someone told him that she was alive, he was very disappointed.

'Yuh feel Florence should rally so long,' Uncle Bogo asked. 'By my calendar she shoulda dead two days ago.'

'Yuh have a calendar?' Saga asked.

'I have that, an' I have a chart about the whereabouts of people who sick bad. Look, I have to go by my cousin in Mamoral. He sick bad-bad. I should be leavin' tonight for Mamoral, but I have to wait on Florence.'

'Is really hard on yuh,' Saga said, wanting to encourage more talk.

'Yes, man. It real hard. An' I don't see why she should get on so. She dead already but she too wicked to lie down an' shut she eyes.'

'Yuh mean yuh like wakes so much, Uncle?' Spiff said.

'Wake is my line,' Uncle Bogo said. 'Some people like stick-fighting, some like wedding, some like carnival an' cricket, but I adore a wake. Wake is my fête. I will go to O-hi-o-ho to a wake. I went Matelot an' Tamana an' Saparia an' Moruga an' Fishing Pond to wake. One night me alone walk through Fifth Company an' went

Moruga. My old boss was dead an' they send an' tell me because they know I had to be there an' it didn't have no truck to carry me. The truck did pass already an' that hour yuh couldn't get car…'

'Yes,' Saga encouraged.

'An I walk. When I tell yuh how uncle walk. But I didn't regret it. That was wake. People bongo till morning, an' the rum an' coffee kept flowing. That was wake! It don't have wake so again.' Uncle Bogo fell silent, thinking.

'So yuh goin' up by Ma Florence now, Uncle?' Doctor said, hoping to start Uncle Bogo talking again.

'I goin' up by Florence, yes. I goin' to see how she shaping. I hope she kick off soon, 'cause is weeks now I waiting on Florence to dead.'

Charleau laughed after Uncle Bogo had moved off, and said, 'Look at that! He love wake. Kill 'im dead so long as he could sing an' drink rum at his own wake.'

Dolphus said, 'That is he. Me, I like me belly.'

'Everybody know that,' Charleau said. 'You will eat yuh throat.'

'I livin' to eat,' Dolphus said. 'I not shame to say it, because I have nothing else to interest me.'

Spiff, an albino, said, 'Hush yuh arse, Dolphus, yuh have no pride.'

'You take yuh pride an' carry it home,' Dolphus said.

'Yuh see me,' Spiff said. 'When I win my sweepstake, I don't want one of you bitches for friend. Yuh too stupid.'

'That's why yuh'll never win a black cent,' Dolphus said.

Spiff laughed. 'Listen!' he said. 'When I win I goin' to keep a big spree for the tesses.'

Dolphus laughed.

Spiff turned to Dolphus. 'Yuh could come, Dolphus, but wash yuh foot when yuh comin'.'

The tesses laughed.

'Talk,' Dolphus said. 'This is a free country. Talk.'

'Yes,' Spiff continued. 'It goin' to be a big fête. Rum like water. Drink, get drunk, behave like ole-nigger, fight and cuss an' eat yuh belly full.' He looked at Dolphus. 'But don't ask me for a penny. I not givin'.'

'I gettin' married to a nice ugly woman – yuh know, like Hog-Mouth Marie, only uglier. I want when people see me passin' with she to say: "Look at Spiff! Yuh mean he couldn'ta get a nicer woman than that?" Me, I don't want no nice woman to worry my brain.'

Dolphus said, 'Spiff, with that face, a female alligator wouldn't want yuh if yuh had a million dollars in gold.'

Spiff said, 'I know somebody who'd want me right now.'

'Who?' Doctor asked.

'That's between Dolphus an' me,' Spiff said. 'Private affairs.'

That same night Clayto, Saga's cousin, stopped his bicycle at the culvert, and Spiff turned on Clayto.

'The bull stallion reach,' Spiff said. 'Where yuh went? The one by the sawmill or the one up by Ma Dovey?'

'Went up the road,' Clayto said, as if he was holding a secret.

Doctor said: 'I know where you went.'

'Don't tell nobody,' Clayto said.

'Somebody goin' to chop off yuh neck for their wife,' Charleau said.

'Don't say that. That's dangerous talk,' Clayto said.

'Okay,' Spiff said. 'How much yuh make tonight?'

'Yuh wouldn't believe me.'

'Yuh know I does believe all yuh lies, Clayto,' Spiff said. 'How much?'

'Five. I slowin' down. Five, and last night six. Yuh see I slowin' down.'

'Whee-ee!' Doctor said, 'yuh's a real bull stallion.'

'What's the most yuh ever make?' Spiff said. Somehow, they always got around to that question.

With a smile, his teeth showing in the half light: 'Nineteen one night,' Clayto said, 'and after, I sleep for two days.'

'Well, Clayto, you can lie,' Spiff said.

Clayto said, 'Don't say that. Yuh's a boy to me. Yuh never even see a woman pee, what yuh tellin' me 'bout life.'

'But yuh know yuh lie, Clayto,' Spiff insisted.

'I don't have nutten more to say,' Clayto said and rode off on his bicycle.

'Why? Why?' Spiff said. 'Clayto does lie so. Why?'

'How yuh know he lie?' Dolphus asked.

'Because he damn well lie, that's how,' Spiff said.

'Why he can't make nineteen?'

'A bull can't make nineteen,' Spiff answered. 'Who's Clayto?'

'Yuh forget he's a bull stallion,' Doctor said.

'He could be a bull ram, he can't make nineteen,' Spiff said.

'What's the most you make?' Dolphus asked Spiff. 'If yuh never had a woman, say so. Don't lie.'

'I don't have to lie. Five. The night I win in the whappie an' went down town. Two on Nelson Street, two on George Street, an' then I stop San Juan by a little thing an' make one more. You remember the night, Doctor?'

'Yes,' Doctor said. 'An' afterwards you nearly puke out yuh guts. An' the taxi-driver charge us extra because you puke in his car.'

'Was the rum,' Spiff said. 'I never drink such bad rum. Three drinks an' I was drunk like a fish an' hot like eighteen Puerto Ricans.'

'That was fête,' Doctor said. 'A woman cry an' tell me how she love me. Imagine! Me, a boy from the bush, havin' me first woman.'

'Love yuh money,' Dolphus said.

'That must be true, 'cause one time I went back there, and sailors was ashore, an' she ask me who I is and I tell she I's the same boy who did come down the time. An' she tell me she don't know me, an' I try to remind she how she say she love me and she tell me I better go quick before she call the man for me.'

'You see. Was yuh money she love,' Dolphus said.

'Woman is bitch,' Doctor said.

'All that is sense,' Dolphus said. 'An' you can't learn that in no high school.'

Yes, that was sense. And Walter remembers it all. And there were other things with sense that he remembers.

Like the time near Christmas when Saga and he and Spiff and Doctor and a whole set of them sat on the culvert one night and decided to make a cook. First, they went into Martin's garden and dug some yams and dasheen, then they went up by Mr Dominic.

Spiff and Doctor, each with a wet bag, crawled into Mr Dominic's yard, and the night was dark and they went right under the lime tree where the chickens roosted. They snatched two plump hens and shoved them into the bags before they could make a cluck; then they all went down by where Spiff stayed in a room in an old house and made a cook right there in the yard. Just as they had finished cooking and were about to begin eating, Mr Dominic, who had travelled late that night, seeing the light and hearing the talking by where Spiff lived, went over and joined the company and was given a share of the meal.

When he tasted the chicken, he asked, 'Who's the cook?'

Saga was the cook, and Mr Dominic complimented him on his culinary ability.

They remained a long time in the yard, cracking jokes and eating, and Doctor piled some green bush on the dying fire to make smoke to keep away mosquitoes. Mr Dominic was so pleased with the meal and the conversation that he sent one of the boys for a bottle of rum. The rum came and brought increased spirit into the company. Mr Dominic became talkative and told the fellows about how it was when he was young, what a good time he and his friends had, how they used to dig people's yams, and steal people's chickens, only in those days it wasn't really stealing.

'Nowadays, fellas can't do that. People not understanding like they used to be,' Mr Dominic said. 'If you go to a man garden and pick a half-ripe orange, the man want the magistrate to lose you in jail.'

Well, that time, with the liquor and the food, jokes, and the tesses in a merry mood, Mr Dominic was enjoying himself immensely; so when the first bottle was nearly dead, he sent for another. Halfway down the second bottle Spiff began giggling, and when he got caught in a spasm of suffocating laughter the reason for which he wasn't able to state, the tesses agreed that Spiff couldn't hold his liquor. They said that Spiff was drunk.

'Can't hold your likker,' Mr Dominic said.

'The man drunk,' Doctor said.

'No,' Spiff said. 'I not drunk.'

'Yuh drunk, Spiff,' Saga said. 'Go inside an' lie down.'

'No,' Spiff argued.

'Well, you not exactly sober,' Mr Dominic said.

'You want to prove I not drunk?' Spiff said.

'Yes. Stand on one leg,' Mr Dominic said. 'If you stand on one leg you good.'

Spiff laughed. 'I don't have to stand on no one leg. I have an easy way to prove.'

'What? Walk on a straight line?' Mr Dominic asked.

'Go an lie down, Spiff,' Saga said.

'I just want to ask one question, an' then you'll know I not drunk. One question.'

'Ask your question,' Mr Dominic said.

Spiff, with an effort, stopped laughing.

'Where,' he asked, 'where we get this yam an' this dasheen to cook?'

'I don't know,' Mr Dominic said.

'Not you. Let them answer.'

'Well…' Doctor hesitated.

'Lissen: we get them by Martin garden, eh? Right or wrong?'

'Right,' Doctor said.

'An' where… where we get the fowl from?'

'Lissen, Spiff,' Saga said. 'Lissen, Spiff… what happen?'

'No,' Doctor said quickly. 'Spiff, you not drunk. You not drunk.'

'I drunk,' Spiff said. 'You-all say I drunk an' I have to prove my integrity. Don't tell me I not drunk. Let me prove it.'

'Spiff,' Doctor said. 'You not drunk. You don't have to prove nothin'.'

'Yes,' Saga agreed. 'Anybody can see you not drunk.'

Spiff laughed. 'Answer my question! Where we get the fowl? Who went for the fowl? I was one that went, and you, Doctor, was one, an' each of us had a wet bag. Right?'

No one answered.

'Right, tesses?'

'I tell you, you not drunk,' Doctor said in a small voice. 'You not drunk.'

'Let me prove it.'

'I mean,' Mr Dominic said, 'let the boy talk. Answer him.'

'You have sense, Mr Dominic. You's the onliest man here that have sense,' Spiff said. 'C'me on, boys, tell me where we get the fowl.'

'Joke is joke, Spiff. But you know you not drunk. What you trying?'

'Why you didn't say that all the time?'

'You know was joke we making,' Dolphus said.

'Don't gimme that,' Spiff said. 'What you say there, Mr Dominic?'

'Well, I don't see why they can't answer you.'

'You hear that, tesses?'

Doctor signalled for Spiff to be quiet. Spiff ignored him.

'Well, I will answer my own question then,' Spiff said.

'I goin',' Dolphus said, and started to get up.

'No. Wait! We get the fowls off a lime tree. Right? If you don't want to answer, I can talk. It have five people in Nuggle with lime trees. Three with lime tree have no fowl. And is not Papy Aime. Solve that.'

'Wait!' Mr Dominic said, jumping to his feet. 'My tree! My fowls!'

'You smart,' Spiff said. 'Now you know I ain't drunk. Gimme a drink.'

And one of the tesses handed the bottle to Spiff and he drank as cool as ever and passed the bottle to Mr Dominic. 'Take a drink, Mr Dominic.'

Mr Dominic was sputtering with anger.

'Take a drink,' Spiff said. 'The chicken was nice.'

'No,' Mr Dominic said, and started to rage about how they were a bunch of thieves, and how he had a good mind to call in the police.

'Well, well,' Spiff said. 'I don't see why you should get vex. You eat the fowl and say it taste nice.'

And as Mr Dominic raged, Spiff laughed.

'I'll call the police,' Mr Dominic said.

Spiff doubled over laughing. 'Who'll you call police for?'

'You. All of you. Thieves!'

'Don't make joke, Mr Dominic. If you call police for we, call for yourself too.' And Spiff began to sing a calypso:

'Himself told himself, you're charged for speeding,
Himself told himself, the policeman lying;
Himself told himself, don't shout,
And the magistrate charged himself for contempt of court.

'That is you,' Spiff said. 'You have to charge and try yuhself, like the magistrate Spoiler sing about. And let me tell you, police not so stupid to lock us up without taking you in too. So you might as well play cool and take a drink.'

But Mr Dominic didn't want a drink. He rushed off in the darkness, grumbling and cursing.

And somehow, although it was real funny, and he, Walter, had laughed along with the tesses, he saw that there was a big meaning glaring from the incident, and that was something for a man to watch and remember and not forget – for Mr Dominic would have made no row if the chickens had come from another yard. He remembers that.

And he remembers Carnival Saturday afternoon a stout Spanish woman came and made Clayto shame right there on the culvert in the junction. Clayto was sitting on the culvert and she went straight up to him.

'Clayto, Clayto, you's a stinkin dog. Yuh see how yuh beat me up an' swell-up me eye an' buss-up me lip? Yuh see what yuh do, Clayto?'

Clayto made no answer.

The woman said, 'I talkin' to you. Tell yuh friends why yuh beat me an' buss-up me lip an' swell-up me eye.'

Clayto said, 'Go from here, woman.'

She said, 'No. Tell yuh friends why yuh beat me up.'

And Spiff and the other tesses who were near by went nearer to hear what the woman had to say.

'Say why yuh beat up the woman, Clayto,' Spiff urged.

Clayto said, 'Woman, I say to go from here.'

'Yuh beat me up, Clayto. Yuh better tell yuh friends why, else I will tell them.'

Clayto said, 'Maria, go home! Go from here!'

The woman said, 'You's a stinkin good-for-nothin' dog. You

ent no kinda man. Yuh have no use to a woman. Listen ev'rybody, Clayto not good. I hear how he does come on the culvert an' boast an' say how he does do woman this an' how he does do woman that. But Clayto don't do woman one thing. He not good.'

Clayto said, 'You goin' to make me lose patience, Maria.'

The woman said, 'Don't call me name. I done with you. Because I get a man who's some good to a woman, yuh come an' beat me up. Yuh not good, yuh hear. Yuh not good, Clayto. An' don't come by my door an' knock again.'

Clayto was a tall, good-looking fellow. He bent his head and got off the culvert and began to walk home, and Spiff, who was sitting right there, shouted after him, 'Clayto! O Clayto! How much yuh make last night? How much?'

Clayto didn't turn back and he didn't answer.

And that night with the dance in the Roman Catholic school, how Ambrose Philip and his Riot Squad played music, and how the guitar man was drunk and he wasn't playing good and Bravay the village bad man went up to the guitar man and cuffed him and punched the guitar and broke it and then walked out of the dance, and how Ambrose Philip didn't want to continue playing, but the tesses said he had to play, or else... And Ambrose played.

That night, there was a short, fat girl with dimples in her cheeks and mischief in her eyes. Whenever Walter danced with her, she clung to him and swung her belly against his thighs, and there was the uneven spasm of her breath on his neck and he became all warm and excited in his clothes, and when the music stopped he had to push his hands in his pockets and walk back to his seat to prevent the others from noticing the effect she had on him. Just before intermission, she turned and winked at him and walked outside and he slipped out behind her and met her waiting by the steps for him, and they walked in the darkness past the cemetery and she kept giggling while he fumbled with her clothes.

And that Carnival Monday morning how it was right there near the shop by the junction. Sixteen stickmen came from Fifth Company to play stick against the men of Nuggle. Among them were Bambara, Margar, Big John and Roe Zolie, the champion

105

stickman who had defeated Maliboo from Moruga the Saturday before. And that was a terrible morning for Nuggle.

The stickmen of Nuggle couldn't stand against the men from Fifth Company. Dolphus got cut, Kepti received a blow to his ribs and couldn't raise his right hand, Parakeet got cut on his chin; only Short Boy drew blood for Nuggle. He cut Bambam on the forehead, but Roe Zolie cracked him on the skull and threw him out of circulation for the remainder of the day.

Not a stickman from Nuggle could shine.

The men from Fifth Company started to chant:

'Tell them to find
Tell them to find a bois man
Tell them to find a bois man
To stand up to we champion.'

Old stickplayers like Mr Regis and Old Colo began to cry when they heard that. Old Colo wanted to go in the ring against the men from Fifth Company, but his friends dragged him away.

And even he, Walter, when he heard the drums and the chanting felt strong and wanted to pick up a stick and go in the ring. And Saga kept telling him to take it easy. So he took it easy and stood and watched and opened his ears and listened.

Dominic said, 'Not a man. Not a man in Nuggle.' He was sad and angry.

'Where Carresar?' someone asked.

'Carresar sick,' someone said.

'Send for Carresar. Oh Gawd, send for a stickman!' Mr Regis said, looking at the men from Fifth Company dancing in the ring. 'If Carresar dying, tell him to come. He's the only man to match them.'

Dolphus went for Carresar.

Carresar was a tall slim fellow with long fingers and a long thin neck. He had dead-looking eyes and he was knock-kneed. He came down the road, walking slowly. People from Nuggle were looking at him. He walked to the edge of the ring and listened to the boastful chanting of the Fifth Company men.

Mr Regis went up to Carresar. 'Yuh reach, Carresar,' Mr Regis said.

'I reach,' Carresar said, 'but I not playing. I sick.'

'Oh Gawd, Carresar, yuh have to play. They cut down everybody from Nuggle. Only you to take shame out we eye.'

The drums beat. The men from Fifth Company changed their lyrics:

> 'Like they can't find
> Like they can't find a bois man
> Like they can't find a bois man
> To match up with we champion.'

Mr Regis started to hum:

> 'Water in me eye
> I crying
> Woe, Woe is me.'

Men from Fifth Company paraded in the ring.

'Oh Gawd!' Mr Regis said, and looked at Carresar.

'I want a stick,' Carresar said.

Carresar was panting and he began to sweat and to sway in time with the drum-beat.

Dolphus went and brought two, and while Carresar was testing them he went and gave the new lyrics for the chant:

> 'Carresar will play
> Carresar will play yuh bois man
> Carresar will play yuh bois man
> Carresar will defeat yuh champion.'

They cleared the ring.

Roe Zolie danced into the empty ring, threw down his stick and jumped out the ring. Carresar threw his stick atop Roe Zolie's. The two men went into the ring and retrieved their sticks. Roe Zolie began to shuffle gracefully about the ring. Carresar tested his stick across his back and then took up his stance.

The drummers began to beat wildly. The stickmen began to chant:

> 'Mama Mama yuh son in the grave already
> Yuh son in the grave already
> Take a towel and band-up yuh belly.'

The two men shuffled in the ring. Roe Zolie aimed the blow at Carresar's head. Carresar barred the blow and went backwards. Roe Zolie smiled. He held his stick over his head. He crouched low.

A man from Fifth Company said, 'Look at Roe Zolie. He so well covered rain can't wet him.'

Carresar went in with a sliding motion. He was looking at Roe Zolie. Roe Zolie shifted his stance, then shifted back. Carresar went in with his sliding motion. Roe Zolie shifted his stance, and as he was about to change back, Carresar smashed his head. Roe Zolie began to bleed.

The men from Nuggle shouted, 'Belle bois! Belle bois, gascon!' and began to jump up gladly.

Old Mr Regis began the new chant:

'Fifth Company lose
Fifth Company lose a bois man
Fifth Company lose a bois man
Fifth Company lose their pouis man.'

Margar jumped in the ring, seeking revenge. He was too wild. As he rushed in, Carresar let him have it. Margar groaned and held his head. That sent the Fifth Company men wild; in a band, they attacked Carresar and started to rain blows on him. That was what started the riot. The stickmen from Fifth Company had to run to the forest. There would have been murder that day if the police hadn't arrived and dispersed the crowd and made a cordon around the men from Fifth Company to allow them to get into their vehicles. Somehow, these things stick in a man's head.

5

'Here's the papers, Walter,' Stephanie says, entering the living-room where her husband, Walter Castle, is seated.

'I don't want 'em now. Where's Carol?'

'She's inside, changing her clothes. You don't want the papers?'

'No. Not now.'

The woman stands, looks at her husband, then walks towards the window.

'Rain's coming again,' she says.

'It will stop,' he answers. 'It always stops.'

'It fell all night. I hope it doesn't fall this evening,' the woman says, turning from the window.

'Why? You going somewhere?' the man asks.

'You mean you forgot we planned to visit my mother this evening?' the wife says, taking the chair next to her husband's.

'Oh,' the man says and sits upright in his chair.

'You're going?'

The man yawns. 'I don't feel like it,' he says. 'But you and Carol can go.'

'You'll stay with the baby?' the woman asks tentatively.

'Not me. Take your child with you.'

'All right. You still have the headache?'

'What headache? Oh! It's all right.'

'Carol got the tablets for you.'

'It's all right,' the man says.

The woman turns her head in the direction of the back door. She holds her head in an attitude of listening. 'Someone's at the door,' she says. 'Carol,' she calls, 'see who's there for me, please.'

From the bedroom the girl answers, 'All right, Stephanie.'

The man is slumped in his chair, like he is thinking.

The woman says in a tender tone, 'Walter, what're you think-ing?'

'I was thinking about Nuggle and the people there. You don't know the place?'

'I passed through Nuggle once when I was a girl.'

'You have to live there to know the people,' the man says. 'You know something, Stephanie?'

'What?'

'It's desire.'

'What is desire?' the woman asks.

'The root of our problems. We want.'

'Isn't it natural to want?'

'Yes. But most of us don't stop to think why we want the things we believe we want. We just scramble madly.'

'Maybe,' the woman says, 'we don't have time. Maybe we're pushed… I mean maybe we have to get things so fast…'

'It's not time. It's a sense of balance, a sense of values which we don't have,' the man says, sitting upright in his chair.

'What's it, Carol?' The woman turns to the girl standing in the doorway.

'Ruben,' the girl says, pulling the edges of her sweater down-wards.

'Ruben who?' Walter asks.

'Mrs Walls's son,' the wife says.

'Oh. That boy.'

'He's a nice boy. He's Carol's boyfriend,' the wife says with a mischievous smile.

'He's not my boyfriend,' the girl says.

'Well, he doesn't come here to talk to *me*.'

'I just talk to him,' the girl says.

'I'm just joking. He's still a nice boy.'

'Who's a nice boy?' Walter asks, as if he hasn't been following the conversation.

'Ruben,' his wife answers.

'I see him with the idle fellows on the street-corners,' the man says.

'Well, you can't stop that. It's all right as long as he stays out of trouble,' the wife says.

110

'Yes. As long as he stays out of trouble. What he wants?'

'He wants to borrow Walter's pliers,' Carol answers.

'Well, give it to him,' the man says.

'I don't know where to look for it again,' the girl says.

'You looked in the box with the tools?'

'It's not there. And I looked in the cupboard. I don't know where to look again.'

'Look in the drawer,' the man says.

'All right,' the girl says, turning to leave the room.

'My sister's growing,' the man says.

'Yes,' his wife answers. 'I was just pulling her leg about the boy.'

'Which boy? Ruben?'

'Yes. I was just pulling her leg.'

Now there is silence. The wind blows into the room, the curtains flap.

'What were we talking about?' Stephanie asks.

'About desire and a sense of values,' the man says. 'You know, I wonder what's really important in this life.'

'Living,' the woman says.

'Yes, and what is living? The people at Nuggle work hard all week and when they get paid on Saturdays, they go to the rum shop, or go and gamble under the old house by Mack. They don't seem to think about doing anything else. And when it's Christmas they want to have their houses stocked with rum, and they want rum for Carnival… There is something in that. There must be some significance in that.'

'Perhaps they don't value money,' the woman says.

'Perhaps they have nothing else to do with money,' the man says. 'Or perhaps that is what living means to them – drinking and gambling. Perhaps that is the meaning they have for life.'

'You mean, having a good time?'

'Yes. And they don't think of tomorrow or yesterday. They don't think they should have a motor car or a big house.'

'They don't think of improving themselves,' the woman says.

'Life, I don't know what you are,' the man says. 'I don't know. Sometimes I think of life as being a race which some of us run and at which some of us look; but I don't know who's running and who's looking on.'

111

'These things you're thinking are hard things. And I'm a simple woman.'

'Maybe it's better a man live like the people at Nuggle.'

'You want to live like them, thinking nothing of tomorrow and of yesterday?'

'Maybe it would be better so. A man is what he has inside of him, not what he has outside.'

'People don't consider you unless you have something outside to show.'

'Are people so necessary?' the man asks.

'So it would appear,' the woman says. 'The world is how it is. Why don't you accept things as they are and try to make your way in the world as it is?'

'Because I'm not sure how things are, and I can't say that I know how the world is.'

'And you're going to try to find out? Many people have spent their lives searching for the answers and they died without finding them.'

'You're very bright this morning, darling,' the man says.

'I wish I was bright. Then I could make you see that the way is right here in this city, among these people.'

'No, you're not so bright. Stephanie, if a man desires nothing, he's not hurt or disappointed when he receives nothing,' the man says.

'But who wants nothing?' the woman asks. 'Everyone wants to be successful.'

'What is success?'

'I'm not *so* bright, Walter.'

'You know something,' the man says. 'It's funny how a man's supposed to fight a battle he doesn't care about, by rules he doesn't know about.'

'What you mean?'

'I mean that I'm supposed to take as important things which some say are important whether I care about those things or not.'

'Things like what?'

'Like money. Like position. Like all the things people find themselves scrambling for.'

'What you trying to do to yourself?' the woman asks. 'Because you didn't get the promotion, you're trying to say that position is not important? From one extreme, you want to move to another?'

'It's not that,' the man says quickly. 'Perhaps I have just come to realize what is important. You know what is important?' he asks.

'What?'

'Whatever a man thinks is important.'

'We are going round in circles,' the woman says.

'We have to. There's no place else to go.'

'I thought you were searching for something.'

'I am still searching.'

'I wish I could help.'

'You know the way you can help.'

'You mean by agreeing to go and live in the country? I knew you'd get at that. We promised to think of it and then discuss it. I haven't had time to give it enough thought.'

'What you waitin' on?' the man asks. 'Christmas?'

'You're snapping again,' the woman says. 'You don't have to snap.'

'I wasn't snapping. I don't want a quarrel. Look, I'd better go inside and lie down.'

'I'm going to finish cooking,' the wife says.

They both stand. One moves towards the kitchen, the other towards the bedroom.

6

In the bedroom now, the man lies down. Ah, Walter, he thinks, you need to find a way out. You must find a way out, otherwise life would mean nothing… Nothing.

He heaps two pillows beneath his head, relaxes and begins to think.

Now in his mind, he is seeing that night there by the junction at Nuggle. At the roadside there were many parked cars, and away from the cars, nearer to the shop, the villagers stood with their faces turned up, looking at the man in the grey suit on the platform lighted with a gas-lamp. There was a big moon in the sky. The speaker on the platform was a member of the new party – the Party of National Importance.

The villagers were silent and attentive. That was the first time that they were hearing the new party. There was no whappie that night, and no gathering on the culvert. Everyone had come to listen because everyone was interested with an interest that went beyond the usual interest rural folk show for what is fashionable or urban. The mood was one not of hope but of expectancy. The villagers stood and listened quietly.

'This is nineteen-fifty-six,' the man in the grey suit was saying. 'This is the twentieth century. This is the modern world. But with all respect to you, with all respect to you and to your efforts, what do we find here at Nuggle?'

The man paused, the villagers sighed.

'Look at your houses! You want better homes. You want electricity. You want a better water supply. You want a secondary school. The nearest secondary school is twenty-nine and one-half miles from this village. You want opportunities for your children. You want a proper post office. You want more roads and better roads. Most of you I know have to walk many miles, long distances to get to your place of work. Most of you have great difficulty in getting your agricultural produce off the lands. Because of the absence of roads or the poor condition of such roads that exist.

'You need a community centre. Every time I pass through this village I see your young men sitting on the culvert. Is it that they want to sit there and indulge themselves in idle conversation? Is it that they prefer to remain idle and leave undeveloped those talents which the Almighty has given to each one of us? Or is it because they have nowhere else to go to? Isn't it a fact that your young men are forced into idleness and vice because they have no facilities? And what about the young ladies?

'You want something better than this. You want something much better than this crude nothing that you have. Make no mistake about it, ladies and gentlemen, Trinidad is not so destitute. Trinidad is not the poorest country in the world. Trinidad can provide better than it is providing for its citizens. There can be better jobs and more jobs and better amenities and more amenities. But we cannot sit down and expect miracles. We cannot sit down.

'Ladies and gentlemen, we have been in a deep sleep here in these islands of Trinidad and Tobago. It is time that we wake up. Like the good old Creole saying, "It is time that we get up an' get."'

The man is serious. There is no hint of a smile on his face. Yet a few persons chuckle and just for a moment this sweeps over the crowd, like a breeze.

'We of the Party of National Importance have come to awaken you. We have come to lift you from slumber and make you aware of your rights and privileges. We will tell you how much you pay your ministers, and what to expect of them. We will tell you how much you pay your civil servants and what you are to expect of them. We will tell you how your money is being spent.

'Gone is our colonial past. We have a right to expect better than we are getting now. We have a right and an obligation to have a say in the affairs of our country. We have a right and a duty to vote the party of our choice. We have a duty to ourselves and to our children. Do not be taken in by bribes. Do not falter in your duty because of unreasonable and unseasonable sentimentality. You have a duty. You have an obligation. This is your country. You pay the taxes. Every time you buy a pound of sugar. Every time you buy a half-pound of salt-fish or a quarter-pound of onions you are paying taxes.

'You have a voice in your country. And the most eloquent exercise of that voice is to return your party, the party with your interests at heart, the Party of National Importance.

'It is a simple exercise, voting. All you have to do is to make a cross opposite the symbol of the candidate of your choice. In this constituency your candidate is Albert Benjamin. He is a man well known to you, a son of the soil, one that knows your needs, one that knows your grievances. And when you vote for Mr Benjamin, you will be voting for your Party, the Party of National Importance.

'Your symbol is the bow and arrow. The bow and arrow was used by our Carib ancestors to hunt, to provide themselves with meat, and to fight, to protect themselves against the enemy. The bow and arrow was used by our African and Indian ancestors on the mother continents in the same way. Today, we use the bow and arrow as our symbol to slay colonialism and ignorance, to slay immorality in public affairs and narrow-mindedness. The bow and arrow is your symbol.'

The man paused as if he had satisfied himself. The people kept looking at him, although he had paused.

'This country, ladies and gentlemen, is awakening. Up and down the length and breadth of these islands we are publishing the facts. Up and down the length and breadth of these lovely islands we are recruiting people from all walks of life to our ranks. Some of them have been abroad to universities, some of them have degrees, but the bulk of them – the bulk of them, ladies and gentlemen – are simple people. Simple, honest people like you people here at Nuggle, who love their country, who love liberty and respect the equality of all men of all races and creeds. These people are moving forward hand in hand with us. We know that you too will move forward with us. We know that you too will join hands with us.

'At the end of this meeting,' the man said in a changed voice, a voice of strength and authority, 'we would like all those among you who are interested in becoming members of this Party to remain. We have Party cards we would like to distribute and we would like to afford you the opportunity of becoming members. Do not be afraid. Do not be ashamed to do your duty. After the meeting, remain awhile. These groups are being set up throughout these islands; we give the people of Nuggle an equal opportunity of associating themselves actively with the work of the Party of National Importance. Thank you, ladies and gentlemen.'

There were the people clapping their hands and nodding their heads. There were the startled dogs at the edge of the crowd, snapping at each other. There was the hum of human voices speaking in loud whispers, and the breasts of villagers rising and falling in excitement. There was a policeman turning to talk to another policeman, and there was another speaker walking from his chair to the microphone amid the sporadic applause of the villagers who had been so attentive to the previous speaker. And there was the fall of the expectant silence upon the crowd and the turning of faces towards the platform and the new speaker.

And after the last speaker had had his say, there was the chairman, a pudgy black man in a cream flannel jacket, saying: 'We thank you... And do not forget to wait for your Party cards.'

Then there were the villagers returning home, walking fast because many of them had to walk far and the hour was late; and there were the visiting members of the Party getting into their cars; and there were the policemen boarding the jeep, and the inspector of police getting into his car; then there was the snore of vehicles' engines as they warmed up and moved off in the cool night with the big moon sliding gracefully across a patch of white clouds.

Clayto remained behind to get a Party card. When he reached home and saw Saga and Walter, he said, 'I thought you woulda wait for a card.'

Saga said, 'Why?'

Clayto said, 'What happen, you don't like the Party?'

Saga said, 'Because a man like the Party, he must join up?'

'You didn't wait for a card either, Walter?'

'Too many people,' Walter said. 'If they're really starting a Party Group here, I could always get a card.'

Clayto said, 'After you fill out this card, it will go to town to Party headquarters for screening an' so on, then it will come back and you'll know if you'll be a member.'

'Yuh have to pay subscription on it?' Saga asked.

Clayto said, 'Anything a man join, he has to pay subscription. We keeping meeting to form the Party Group next week. We'll elect officers.'

'You might get a big post, Clayto,' Saga said. 'Yuh might even be a big shot in the Party just now.'

Clayto smiled with all his teeth filling his mouth, as if he had said something funny.

'What yuh say, Clayto?' Saga prodded.

Clayto said, 'Who knows? The only man that get a card before me was Soscie. I was second in the line and after Soscie get his, I get mine.'

'Soscie could go far in this politics business,' Saga said. 'He could talk good. If he had education like Mr Reggie, he could reach the top.'

'Yes,' Clayto agreed. 'He's a good boy.'

That night, Clayto was so excited about the Party of National Importance and at the prospect of his being a member that he didn't want to go to sleep and he kept them awake until very late, talking about politics. And the following morning, with the chill breeze and the mist, he continued from where he had left off. And it was not he alone. All the villagers were talking excitedly about the Party and the coming elections. Even when they were coming down from the forest on the truck in the evening the subject had still not been exhausted.

Clayto and Saga and Soscie and Mr Reggie were on the truck. Mr Clyde, the big six-foot Baptist preacher with the voice of a bull, was there too. Although the others were doing a great deal of talking, Mr Reggie kept silence because he was a learned man and had spent many years in Venezuela and in the diamond mines of British Guiana and frequently wrote letters to the *Trinidad Gazette* and was a friend of the schoolmaster in the Roman

Catholic school and his hair was almost completely white and a learned man did not indulge himself in aimless talk or else the people soon ceased to give him the respect to which his intelligence entitled him.

That time, coming down from the forest in the evening, with the old truck clanging over the rough road and the engine singing a hard song climbing the difficult hills, Soscie said, 'Mr Reggie, you was there last night?'

Mr Reggie waited a while and then answered, 'Yup. I was there.'

And the people on the truck fell silent, waiting for Mr Reggie to say more.

'Yup, I was there,' Mr Reggie repeated; and the truck was singing a hard song in a high voice as it went up a big hill.

'And what you think of the Party, Mr Reggie?' Soscie said. Soscie was one of the very few young men in Nuggle that did not gamble, and drank only a little. He had married and had built his own little house and put a galvanized iron roof upon it.

Mr Reggie smiled. It was a habit of his to wrinkle his already lined face into a smile whenever he was asked a hard question.

'You tell me what you think, Soscie,' Mr Reggie said, looking around the truck and letting his eyes linger on Mr Clyde and Clayto.

'Well... well, I think they're good, Mr Reggie. I think they doing a good job educating the people and putting them on the path to progress. And I think they will win the elections.'

Mr Clyde said, 'Long ago we didn't know what happening in Trinidad.'

Soscie said, 'That's true, Mr Reggie.'

Mack, a big bushy-headed fellow sitting in the corner, said, 'I didn't even know I was a taxpayer.'

Mr Reggie said, 'You know now.'

Soscie said, 'We was sleeping and we wake now. But tell us what you think, Mr Reggie.'

'You know I've lived in Venezuela, and was a long time in the mines in British Guiana bush...'

'Yes,' Soscie said. 'Yes.'

'And many times there in the jungle, the law was a man and his strength and his brain and his knife. I know that. And I've seen natives naked as fish in the big river, and I've seen natives in the towns, with clothes on, the civilized ones.'

Soscie looked puzzled.

'Well, last night I heard the politicians offering something and I saw you taking it. But in taking it, you also gave up something… I am puzzling you? Yes. I am puzzling you,' Mr Reggie said with a smile.

'Yes, Mr Reggie,' Soscie said.

'Think. What were you offered?' Mr Reggie asked.

'Opportunities for advancement, better amenities, progress,' Soscie said.

'You can call all that by one name,' Mr Reggie said. 'Desire. You begin to desire. With desire comes knowledge and with knowledge comes the realization of one's limitations, the extent of one's ignorance. You begin to develop a new set of values. You begin to see your nakedness and to curse it,' Mr Reggie said.

Mr Clyde, the big six-foot Baptist preacher, said in his booming voice: 'The Lord said unto Adam, eat of the fruit of all the trees in the garden, but of the trees of wisdom and of life, eat not the fruit thereof.'

'Desire!' Soscie tested the word on his lips.

'I do not know which is worse,' Mr Reggie said, 'desire or ignorance. Which do you think is worse, Soscie?'

'I cannot tell you,' Soscie said. 'Which do you think?'

'The end of desire is frustration, and even more than frustration, there will be, along the way, fear and hate and cut-throat competition. That is the price you pay for so-called advancement. That is the price of your progress.'

'Is it too great a price?' Soscie asked.

'You tell me, Soscie.'

'We must pay it. The times are like that, Mr Reggie.'

'I have seen the natives, the bush people, naked as the fish in the big river, and I've seen them in serge jackets in the heat of the sun in the city. That is innocence and that is civilization,' Mr Reggie said.

'Mr Reggie, you not blaming the Party for opening the eyes of the people?' Clayto asked.

'No, Clayto. I don't blame the Party. I only note that where there was innocence there is now desire, and I have a fair idea of what will follow.'

'And behold, after Adam and the woman had eaten of the forbidden fruit, they went and dressed themselves in leaves.' Mr Clyde lifted his voice above the clanging of the truck and said the words as he might have said them to a congregation in the Baptist church on a Sunday morning.

'The world is progressing,' Soscie said, 'and we must go with it. What else can we do?'

'Progress is a word,' Mr Reggie said. 'A word we think we know the meaning of.'

There was silence that time in the truck. When the truck stopped for Mr Reggie to get out, Soscie remembered and said, 'Mr Reggie, you haven't told me what you think of the new Party.'

'I haven't told you?' Mr Reggie asked, getting off the truck slowly that time, for he was no longer a young man.

Soscie said nothing, and the truck moved off and left Mr Reggie standing at the roadside.

Afterwards, in the truck, the conversation shifted to Mr Reggie. The villagers said that he was brighter than the school-master in the Roman Catholic school. Some said that he had been a politician in Venezuela. Some said he had been to prison in Dutch Guiana. They all agreed that he was a learned man.

The night after the general elections, villagers flocked to Miss Bertha's parlour to listen to the results of the elections over the radio.

It was like listening to boxing from America with Joe Louis fighting, or like listening to cricket from Australia with the West Indian team playing. Around the radio, men were glued to their seats, and the doorway of the parlour was jammed with people, and even out in the streets the restless ones moved up and down, taking in the news as it was relayed to them. Oh, there was noise and excitement, so much so that Miss Bertha threatened to close the parlour and go to bed if the people couldn't restrain themselves. They promised to be less noisy, and in fact, there were a few moments of quiet, but as soon as a result was announced, voices rose in support or in condemnation. All that night the villagers waked to hear the results, and when the first preliminary count revealed that the Party of National Importance had captured the majority of seats, the villagers listening sent up a great hurrah which Miss Bertha joined rather than attempted to contain.

That night, the tesses went home in a singing, shouting band, and on the following day Clayto declared a holiday and didn't go to work. He had been elected treasurer of the Nuggle Party Group. Soscie was secretary and Dominic was elected president. That day, Clayto and other Party members and well-wishers remained in the rum shop drinking, making merry and congratulating each other on the victory of their Party.

Then, about two weeks afterwards, a member of the central Party in Port of Spain arrived at Nuggle and spoke to the Party Group members. The meeting was held in the old Friendly Society hall. Saga and Walter attended.

'Do not think that we have formed these Party Groups only for the elections. Do not think that now we have won the majority of seats in the legislature and formed the government that your work here in this Party Group and in other Party Groups throughout these islands has come to an end. You must not for one moment indulge yourself in this sort of thinking.

'Rather, you must think that your work, like the work of the new government, has just begun. It is not only that we must consolidate our position, it is not only that we must congratulate ourselves on our victory, it is not enough for us to say that we have been supporters of this government; now, we must approach our civic duties with a greater sense of responsibility and a greater sense of dedication. Now, we must be prepared to make every effort to assist the central government in its programme of development.

'Being a member of a Party Group at this time brings with it new and perhaps strange responsibilities. It certainly involves added work. But there is this: you have a better opportunity to get closer to your government, to make your government aware of your problems, and to help your government solve the problems of the country. You are in a position now to tell us where you think we are going wrong – in fact, to guide us. And so that you carry out this exercise expeditiously, it is necessary for you to observe the workings of your government. And when I say your government, I do not only mean your ministers and members of the legislature, I mean also your civil servants, I mean also labourers employed on government projects – *your* projects.

'If I might say this,' the man added. 'You must realize that we are a young government and we ask you not to expect miracles in a short space of time. Nevertheless, this must not deter you from bringing to the attention of the government, what you consider to be problems which affect you.

'I must thank you again, on behalf of myself and on behalf of the central Party, for the great part you have played in our victory. A victory that is as much yours as it is ours. We know that we can always expect the unstinted efforts of the people of Nuggle in our support.'

The villagers cheered; the villagers clapped their hands and slit their faces with their smiles.

One evening Walter went by Miss Bertha to listen to the news over the radio, and he picked up the day's newspaper and happened to see an advertisement calling for departmental clerks in the government service. He showed it to Saga.

'Good,' Saga said. 'If I was you I'd apply.'

'You think that would make sense? Most of the jobs you see advertised are already taken. If you want to get a job, you must have contact on the inside,' he said.

'If I was you I'd apply,' Saga said. 'It won't cost you more than a sheet of paper and a three-cent stamp to try. If you lucky, you get through; if you not lucky, what you lose?'

He took Saga's advice and applied for the job.

On the same day the letter was acknowledged, Clayto came home with his face set up like rain in the sky.

'You know what happen?' he said.

'What?' Saga asked.

Instead of answering Saga's question, Clayto ground his teeth and said, 'I don't know how the hell they expect a man to live now.'

'What happen? What happen?' Saga wanted to know.

'They crazy,' Clayto said. 'They more than crazy!'

'You eating up yuhself an' I don't know what yuh talkin' about,' Saga said. 'What happen?'

'They want to give a man one licence a year to stamp wood. One nasty licence with five hundred cubic feet of wood. How a man goin' to live on that?'

'A man not bound to live on that,' Saga said.

'What he goin' to do?' Clayto wanted to know.

'He could die on it,' Saga said.

'You damn right. A man could die on it if he want. But I tell you, something have to happen. Something must happen. This thing can't go so,' Clayto said. 'Tomorrow I have an appointment with the Forest Ranger and I will find out from him what they intend to do. You will hear. You will hear.'

'Chut!' Saga said. 'You wouldn't do a thing. You's just a blow-hard.'

'Blow-hard eh? Blow-hard? Tomorrow you'll hear me an' the Ranger.'

'I'll come with you,' Saga said. 'We'll go with him, eh, Walter.'

On the following day, while they were going to the forest on the truck, the woodworkers kept grumbling that the arrangement by which a man was granted only one licence carrying five hundred cubic feet of wood for one year, was unreasonable, impossible, and that something should be done about it.

Some of them had appointments with the Forest Ranger that morning and they longed to meet him to tell him their opinion on the matter.

The Forest Ranger was already there when they arrived. He went up to the group with which he had been appointed to work and read out the names to make certain that they all were there: Clayto, Soscie, Mr Reggie, Mike and Mack. When the Forest Ranger came in the midst of the men to arrange the order in which the stamping of the wood would be carried out, Soscie touched on the subject nearest to the hearts of those present.

'I don't know how a man going to live on five hundred cubic of wood for one whole year,' he said. 'Five hundred cubic. You pay eight cents a cubic for the wood – that is forty dollars. You pay the workman twenty cents a cubic to fall the tree and cross-cut it

– that is a hundred dollars. You pay twenty-five cents a cubic to the tractor to pull out the wood from the forest and put it by the roadside for the truck to take it – that is a hundred and twenty-five dollars. That is two hundred and sixty-five dollars. And when you sell, you get eighty cents a cubic. I don't know how a man going to live on that for a whole year.'

The Forest Ranger said, 'I have orders. One licence to a man. Five hundred cubic feet to a licence. I have orders.'

Clayto said, 'And the wood so far inside the forest. Long ago a man could make five–six trips with a tractor; now he making one in the morning and one in the evening, and he lucky. A man have to pay instalments on the tractor. A man have to eat. You have to eat something solid when you doing this kinda hard work.'

Mack said, 'And some special people getting the best wood nearby… Those people who could afford it.'

'You know what you saying, Mack?' the Forest Ranger said.

'How yuh mean if I know what I saying? Some people always getting appointment before everybody else and getting the best wood and the wood nearest to the roadside. Things don't happen so. That don't happen so,' Mack said.

'Somebody must be first,' the Forest Ranger said.

'I know,' Mack said, 'but why I never first? Why I always behind?'

'Look,' the Forest Ranger said, 'let's start stamping the wood.'

'And as to this one licence business,' Mack said, 'that is shit.'

'I have my orders. If you want more wood, go down to the office and put your case to the conservator. I can't do one thing about it.'

'The last time we went by the conservator, he tell us about how the forest is not to cut down. He well off, living nice, could say anything; but he telling we who living off the forest that the forest can't cut down,' Soscie said.

The Forest Ranger said, 'I know all you want wood, but you can't make the forest a savannah, either. The forest is here not only to provide timber. The forest has many other uses.'

Clayto said, 'The best thing is to see the Minister in charge of forestry. Form a delegation and go and see him.'

'I don't mind what you do,' the Forest Ranger said. 'I have

orders and I can't go against orders. If they say five hundred to a man, I'm giving five hundred. If they say stamp out the whole forest, I'm stamping it out. But they didn't say stamp out the whole forest; they say five hundred cubics to one man.'

Mack said gruffly, 'I'm a Party member.'

The Forest Ranger looked at him.

'I'm a Party member and Party members should have preference,' Mack said.

'I don't know that,' the Forest Ranger said. There was a tightening in his voice. 'I don't know that at all.'

'Who you think pay the civil servants?' Mack asked. 'We pay them. Our taxes.'

'Carry your politics by the junction,' the Forest Ranger said. 'I don't want any part of it.'

'You don't want to hear me, eh? I bet I get you transferred. Rangers like you only interested in one set of people – those who have something to grease yuh hands. Fellas like you shouldn't be in the Service at all,' Mack said.

'I don't think I have to take that kind of talk from you, Mack. I don't think I have to take that kinda talk from any licencees,' the Forest Ranger said.

Mack was a big-chested, bushy-headed fellow. 'I'm goin' to see 'bout you,' he said.

'Look,' the Forest Ranger said, 'Mr MacDonald, if you continue like this I'm not going to work for you today.'

Mack said, 'Do what you want, you bound to work for me. That's what you gettin' paid for. I paying you. My money paying you. My taxes.'

'Well, Mack,' the Forest Ranger said, 'I'm not going to work for you today. I won't take your insults. Make a new appointment. Make a report. Do what you want. I'm not working for you today.'

'What?' Mack said.

'You heard me. I'm not taking your insults. Who's first?' he said, turning to the others. 'Let us go.'

Mack's chest began to heave and Mack began to curse.

That evening they finished stamping wood late and the trucks had already left for Nuggle, so they had to walk down, except the Forest Ranger who had his motorcycle.

'Soscie,' Mr Reggie said while they were going down that evening, 'that is the use to which you intend to put your Party card?'

'You mean the thing with Mack and the Forest Ranger, Mr Reggie? That was Mack. The other Party members didn't say anything.'

'I was waiting, expecting one of you to rebuke him.'

'We couldn't do that, Mr Reggie.'

'Why not? He was far out of place.'

'A man can't keep his family on five hundred cubics of wood for a whole year, Mr Reggie. And it's true that some Rangers have their partisans who get the best wood near the roadside,' Soscie said.

'That is not the point,' Mr Reggie said. 'Mack was out of place.'

'Well, maybe Mack was wrong,' Soscie said. 'But a man can't live on five hundred cubics. I think we'll have to go to the Minister for Forestry.'

'This Party card,' Mr Reggie said. 'This Party card.'

'What's with the Party card?'

'This Party card can be rum,' Mr Reggie said. 'A strong drink to stimulate you to action. But you can become so drunk on it that you could believe that you could whip the world. But when the effect wears off… There is that time when the effect of the liquor wears off. You have to guard against that time, Soscie.'

'It's Mack,' Soscie said.

'Too many Macks,' Mr Reggie said. 'Too many Macks expecting something for nothing, expecting to have things the easy way. Too many Macks taking this Party card as something to wear in their buttonhole.'

'You think so, Mr Reggie?'

'Look,' Mr Reggie said. 'If there was another Mack there this morning, can you imagine what would have happened?'

'There was only one Mack, Mr Reggie.'

'Yes. But there might be too many Macks in Trinidad and Tobago, and then what?'

'You sound sad, Mr Reggie,' Soscie said.

'I am sad, boy, for I am seeing something that is sad to see. Sad-sad to see.'

'What, Mr Reggie?'

'The death – no, not the death, but the strangulation of the individual. I see not men, not individuals, but Party cards and badges.'

'That is the only way for the people to have a say in the government, Mr Reggie,' Soscie said.

'Yes,' Mr Reggie said, 'and it is that that saddens me; for men in mobs are less than men.'

'The Party Group is not a mob,' Soscie said quickly.

'Now it is not,' Mr Reggie said. 'But I have seen too many things not to see beyond this day. And I am an old man and afraid of what is strange. Already I see hard times are with us.'

And it was true. Hard times had arrived at Nuggle. Woodcutters found less employment, tractor-drivers had less work, and some persons, like Clayto, who had taken out their own tractors on the instalment plan found it difficult to meet the monthly instalments and get by, and they lived always in dread of having their tractors seized. A whole series of unsatisfactory reactions had set in. Villagers of Nuggle began to know what it meant to be really poor: the men began to know what it was to go without a drink or a smoke, and big tesses who used to bet five and ten dollars on a card or on the fall of dice knew the humiliation of betting a shilling at a time. All these things overtook Nuggle quickly. And when, one evening, Miss Bertha, the postmistress, called Walter and gave him a brown envelope marked O.H.M.S. which, when he opened it, said that he should report for the job for which he had applied some months previously, he was glad. He showed it to Saga.

'I glad for you, boy,' Saga said. 'You'll be leaving Nuggle now.'

'Yes.'

'And to think,' Saga said, 'I was thinking of leaving this place next month. Things getting too hard. Now you going I will leave quicker.'

'How long we spent here?' Walter asked Saga, as if he didn't know.

'Two years.'

'Two years!'

'Yes. Time does fly. And you liked the place?'

'Yes. I liked it.'

'All good things…'

'… come to an end,' Walter added.

'Yes. I'll be coming to town right behind you. I have some calypsos to sing when calypso tent open.'

'I hope you get through with your calypsos.'

'All I want is a chance to sing.'

'I know you'll get through, Saga.'

'Boy, I know I'll try like hell.'

'We'd better go and tell Clayto the news. You think he'll be sorry?'

'Clayto will be glad for you, but he might be sorry we leaving – you know how?'

'Yes. Well, let's go and tell him.'

7

'Walter,' the wife calls from the doorway. 'It's time for lunch.'

'I'm not hungry.'

'Carol's ready to eat and I'm ready.'

'Well, go ahead. I'm not hungry.'

'I'm not going to eat until you come.'

'What's the matter? Am I that important?' He begins to get off the bed.

When he reaches the living-room, his wife and sister are already seated at the table. The man sits and his wife begins to uncover the dishes.

'Again!' the man exclaims. 'Red beans again!'

'But I thought you liked them, Walter.'

'Well, doo-doo-la, I don't like 'em.'

'Very well, I won't buy any more. Carol,' she says, turning to the girl, her husband's sister, 'you see how much trouble a husband can give?'

The little sister smiles timidly.

'I don't like red beans,' Walter says. 'I just don't like them.'

'Well, I won't cook them again. I thought you said you wanted them. I think it was a Sunday or two ago you said, "What! Don't they sell things like red beans any more…?" I just thought you liked them. I just thought…'

'All right. You don't have to get vexed for that,' the man says.

'I'm not getting vexed. I'm just explaining.'

'What's there to explain? I don't like the beans. That's all.'

'All right, Walter. All right.'

They settle down to eating. The cutlery begins to make music on the plates and jaws begin to swing on hinges. But there is, at the table, something like uneasiness, like apprehension; something like a cloud.

The man eats, his eyes are looking into the plate before him; the wife eats, her eyes are looking also at her plate; the little sister eats hurriedly, looking into her plate, anxious to finish and be off elsewhere where the atmosphere is less tense, the mood less severe.

From the adjoining apartment there are sounds of a scuffle: now there is a scream, and another scream, and another still louder scream.

The man looks up from his plate; the woman looks up from her plate; the little girl looks up from her plate; they do not look at one another.

The scuffle continues next door. The man breaks the silence. 'Bolo and his wife fighting for food again.'

'Every Sunday,' his wife says.

'But can't they skip just one Sunday?' the little sister asks.

'Bolo has a big appetite and Bolo's wife has a big appetite.'

'Perhaps she doesn't cook enough,' the little sister ventures.

Now the husband is smiling, and for a moment, it looks as if this thing, this cloud, will go from the table.

The wife smiles also, but she cannot resist the temptation to make an observation.

'At least they know why they're fighting,' she says.

'Meaning?' the husband asks. 'Meaning what?' And though his tone is mild, there is something behind the question.

Once more the temptation is irresistible to the wife.

'Meaning,' the woman says, 'that some people bicker for no apparent reason.'

Now it is done. Immediately the woman wishes that she had not spoken. Now she prays hard that her husband will let it pass. But it is no use, such a prayer, for her husband lifts his eyes to hers.

'There are always reasons,' he says. 'Always.'

She need not reply, but she must straighten things out, she must bring the subject on the right track.

'Apparent reasons?' she asks. 'Why do we always quarrel?' she adds in a tone of compromise.

'I guess we do not see eye to eye often enough,' the man says, one pitch higher than the tone in which she spoke.

Now there is silence at the table, except for the clinking of knife and fork on plates. And now the little sister, with an air of triumph, finishes her lunch, asks to be excused and rises from her seat, glad that the threatening cloud has not burst in her presence.

A few moments pass.

'Have you decided, Walter?' the wife asks, unsteadily.

'No. Not yet. Have you?'

They eat on in a strained silence loud with their thoughts.

'Do you think it's such a good thing, really?' the woman ventures timidly. 'I mean leaving and going to the country with the baby and the one inside me here. And what will become of Carol?'

He doesn't answer. If the woman would raise her head and look at the man's face, she would see that he is struggling with something, and she wouldn't press him. But she does not raise her head. She is looking at a bit of meat at the edge of her fork.

'After all, this – this is our life. This is my life too. You're my husband, I'm your wife.'

'What book you read that outa? "This is my life too… You're my husband, I'm your wife." Where you got that?' he asks, his tone crisp and short.

'I didn't read it out of any book.'

'You thought it up all by yourself? Great! My wife is great. "You're my husband, I'm your wife!" You know what that means?'

The woman hesitates.

'No. I bet you don't. The words sound pretty and you say them…'

'I don't understand. I just don't understand what you're trying to get. I should understand. I have a right to understand.'

'Sure. You're my husband – I mean wife, I'm your husband, eh? Sure.'

'Make fun of me,' the woman says. 'But you can't change the world.'

'I cannot change the world. But I can change my world. That's enough for me. I can get outa the race.'

'No, Walter,' she says. 'No.' Now she looks into his eyes. She looks as if she has stumbled upon something. The man senses it.

'What you mean?' he says softly, apprehension creeping into his voice.

'You are in the world, Walter. You're caught in the race like anyone else.'

'Yes. And I want to get out. What's wrong with that?'

'It's too late, Walter.'

'How can it be too late? What you mean?'

'Walter… you see… you see, you can't take from the world and not pay. You cannot take one part and reject the other.'

'What have I taken from the world, woman? What?'

'You have a wife. You have a child and you expect another…'

'You?'

'Yes. In a sense I am something that you have taken from the world. That puts you in the race. Before you were married, you could have broken away, gone and lived like a hermit if you wanted. Look, Walter! I would have gone with you but…'

'But! But what? The children?'

'Yes, the children. It would not be fair to them.'

'What wouldn't be fair to them? What is there in this city except hustling and scheming? And here in this Webber Street, what is there but violence and anger and fear?'

'If that is the world,' the woman says, 'then that's the world. Accept it. Fight it if you want to, but accept it, for your own sake, for my sake, for the sake of the children. This is all the world there is here.'

'Fight? Since you're so bright, tell me a way to fight the corruption and the wickedness and the violence in this town.'

'You don't have to fight the whole town.'

'Okay, well, tell me how to fight the corruption where I work and the violence and the fear right here in Webber Street. Tell me.'

She makes no reply.

'Tell me,' the man insists.

'If I could tell you that, I'd be the Minister of Home Affairs.'

'So you can't tell me?'

'No, I can't tell you,' she cries, as if she is about to dissolve into tears.

'Assuming that what you say is true – I mean, about how you and the children are part of the world and that whatever a man takes from the world he must repay; assuming that all that is true, you still cannot tell me that there is anything here in this city. There is nothing here. It is only hustling and scheming and fear, and there is no way to fight them.'

'I didn't say there was no way to fight them. I said that I didn't know the way.'

'Good. You don't know the way to fight those things. I don't know the way. Nobody knows the way. And yet we must remain here.' He draws out his chair and begins to rise from the table.

'There must be something, Walter.'

'What?'

'Perhaps you can't see it, Perhaps I can't see it. But there must be… Can't be all that barren.'

'You cannot see it, I cannot see it. I never met anyone to see it,' the man says. 'What can there be?'

'I don't know.'

'Let's leave this town, Stephanie. We can escape while we have time. We're still young.'

'Escape?' the woman says, looking up at him. 'Escape to what? You say you're escaping from the world. What are you going to?'

With all his heart and strength and intelligence, the man would like to answer that question.

'What am I going to?' he asks, stalling, thinking.

'Yes, Walter. What are you going to?'

What am I going to, the man thinks. In his mind he sees the countryside so quiet. The earth is wet, and the grass is green and glistens with dew and sunlight. The corn is tall and the ears are long, and blonde hair hangs out from the tassels. Birds are singing in a mango tree, the mist is disappearing, the chickens rush for feed and scatter when the dog jumps. The cow is being milked and the potatoes are being hoed and there is a big pumpkin under the avocado tree. Smoke comes from the wood fire and rises to the blue sky. The children bathe in the river and lie down on the bank and laugh, or look at the silver water running over the smooth stones on the riverbed and wait for the coscorob to glide out from beneath the stone. The wind rushes, trees lean and shake; the doves coo and walk on the ground, in pairs.

Words. Words. He has no words to paint the picture that his heart can comprehend.

The man hesitates. The man is afraid even to try, because he knows that he cannot explain what he feels, nor paint what his vision reveals to him.

The wife sits with her face turned up, looking at him, waiting on him.

The man speaks. He is choking. 'Stephanie,' he says. 'We will remain with this nothing. We will remain in this city.'

She is looking at him, waiting. There is something she expects him to add.

'Don't ask me if I will go back to the job now. Don't ask me that one.' He turns and walks towards the bedroom.

'Walter.' Her voice halts him.

'Yes?'

'I love you.'

'Thanks,' he says drily, and continues into the bedroom where he throws himself upon the bed.

All this time he is thinking how a man has to pay: pay for the goods he uses; pay the world for its women and its children and the morsel he scrapes in sweat with his fingers. He had not thought of it that way. He must have been blind not to have seen that there is no other way but to fight in the world as it is, with the people as they are, with the resources at his disposal.

So this world is mine, he thinks. And this land is mine and the people here are my people, and the things that are done in this city – I also am responsible for them. I am one with the land and I am one with the people.

What to do now? What is there to be done, he thinks. What have I done? What have I ever done? Got married? Sired a girl-child? What?

Better go to sleep, he thinks. You did nothing. What can you do except look on and hope that things turn out right for yourself? What can any man do? Who does anything in the world? Better go to sleep and forget all this jazz about fighting the people and fixing the world. People who can help do nothing. So what can you do? Better go to sleep and dream about your balls for the last time. And tomorrow, go and pawn them and hope you're able to redeem them some day. Yes. Better go to sleep or get drunk or something, because that woman, that wife of yours, done knocked the pins from under that grand idea of going to live in the country. She's right and you're crazy to think that running away will solve your problems. A man has to fight right where he finds himself or lie down and let them walk over him. Yes. Better say thank God you have a smart woman who can think with her brains. Better say thank God and go to sleep. She has reason on her side. What do you have to match against reason? Disgust? Fear? Anger? Man, you're crazy to think about dragging that poor pregnant woman and that small child somewhere behind God's back away in the country. Man, you're real crazy. Yes. Better go to sleep.

But the man does not go to sleep. He thinks of Nuggle. What had he done there? Two years! He knew how the people walked in the evening and he knew what they did for a living. He could write a book about the tesses under the old house by Mack, and about up in the forest with axes and cross-cuts, and about the drunkards under the mango tree on Saturday night, and about how Christmas was there at Nuggle, and about how Carnival was; but what had he *done*? He had looked on, looked on like it was a book he was reading, moved by the language, and then he had closed the book. How many books had he closed? There was one at Nuggle. There were others before and there were others after.

8

That day he was leaving Nuggle he stood at the junction, waiting for conveyance to Port of Spain, and looked at the village. Little had changed. Things had just aged. Aged, not grown.

Saga said, 'Two years.'

'It was good,' he said.

'Yes. I'll be coming down next two weeks.'

'You know where to find me? Belmont, by my sister. If I'm not there, look for me on the job. You know where that is?'

'Laventille.'

'Yes.'

'Well, take care of yuhself,' Saga said.

'Right-o. You take care. I want to hear you win calypso king competition next year.'

'All I want is a chance to sing. When you good, they can't stop you.'

'And you good?'

'I tell myself that all the time. Somebody have to tell me that, so I tell myself.'

'You're great.'

'The greatest. No joke.'

'I'll tell the Mighty Sparrow to watch out. The Lord Saga's after his crown.'

'Do that. Look, a taxi.'

'It have room?'

'Look so. Yes. Somebody dropping out. Next two weeks I'll see you. Belmont?'

'Yes. You know the street?'

'Have it cold here in me brain, an' if I forget I have it write down home.'

'Good. All right, see you.'

'Okay, boy.'

He closed one book there when he left Nuggle. And after that?

That same evening, going up by his sister Ruth, he met Carmen, his big sister, wearing a black dress and looking drawn and unhappy. She was about to step in a taxi, but he called her and she turned and, seeing that it was her brother, turned from boarding the taxi.

'Boy!' Carmen said. And she didn't appear capable of saying any more.

They stood there on the sidewalk, looking at each other.

'What about the baby?' he asked. 'What about Clem?'

Her face took on a tragic look. 'The baby's all right. You know I have two of them now. They're all right.'

'And Clem?'

'Clem? Clem…' she began, fighting hard to control her voice. 'Clem dead.'

'What?'

'Clem dead,' she said, swallowing.

'Clem. Dead?'

'Yes, Clem well dead. Five months an' three days since Clem dead and I still can't believe it. I still can't believe Clem dead. You hear about accidents, you read about accidents, you even see them, but you don't know how it is when somebody belonging to you meet his death on the road. Clem leave the house good-good and go and meet his death on the road in an old motor car.'

'I sorry, Carmen. It's sad for you.'

'Sad. More than sad. More than anything.'

'And how you making out?'

'All right. Clem was a man like to have a good time, but he had an eye to the rainy day. I making out all right, and his family – his mother and them – very kind to me. I can't complain. You must come down by me in Point. And how you keeping?'

'All right.'

'Where you going with that grip now?'

'Up by Ruth.'

'Tell she howdy for me. I was to pass up there but time does

138

fly so much I couldn't make it. And what about Ma and the others?'

'I don't know.'

'How you mean, don't know?'

'Well, you see, I wasn't home. I was in the country up at Nuggle. Two years now I haven't been home.'

'No, Walter. That's not good. You must go home. Don't mind what happen, you must go home.'

'All right.'

'I'm glad to see you, though. You looking well. Look, boy, it's getting dark already and I have to reach home so I can't stay to talk to you as I want.'

'That's all right. Say howdy to the children for me.'

'Yes, I have to go. Look, keep well.' Carmen kissed him hurriedly on the cheek. 'I gone,' she said, stretching out a hand to stop a taxi.

'All right, Carmen.'

And afterwards he took a taxi and went up to Belmont by his sister Ruth. He knocked softly on the door. Ruth came quickly and opened the door. He noticed that she was pregnant.

'Walter! Walter!'

'Yes, Ruth. How you?'

Ruth shook her head from side to side. She was his favourite sister.

'Come inside. Come in. Lester!' she called. 'Look, Walter come!'

Lester came and shook hands with him.

'But look how this boy come big!' Ruth exclaimed. 'Where you get all that size from? Where you was? You know, you didn't do so good, staying away so long without sending word about what happening to you. But look at this boy!' She backed off a few paces and looked at him from head to toe.

'Ruth, let the boy siddown first,' Lester said.

'Yes, siddown. Take a seat. Here! Look how this boy come big!' He sat down.

'Now let's hear all the happenings. Where you was?'

And he told how he had been up at Nuggle for two years and how he had worked in the forest there and that he had just come down to Port of Spain because he had obtained employment at the Works Department and was supposed to go to take up work from Monday morning.

'So you want to remain here?' Ruth said.

'If you could put me up for the time being.'

'Just the other day Andrew ask me for you. So you want to remain here? Okay. The neighbours move out so we have the whole house now. We have a spare room there, Lester,' she said, turning to her husband. 'We can let him remain in the spare room.'

'Yes,' Lester agreed.

'Good. Walter, is more than two years since I see you. Well, look at that! Look at that!'

That night he slept there and continued to remain there afterwards. There it was. He was back in the city.

And now he remembers how happy he felt to get a job there in the city, to be there, walking, part of the huge creature with thousands of pairs of swinging hands and lifted feet and bent elbows and crooked knees; how happy he felt to be part of that animal, a cell of the animal, working, and then, at the end of the fortnight, receiving his wages in a brown envelope with his name typewritten upon its face.

What had he done after that?

Some evenings he went to the cinema and some evenings he walked home slowly, passing before department stores and looking at the wares in the showcases. Once he wanted to buy a camera; for two years he wanted to buy a camera. Somehow, he never bought the camera. So he forgot about it. Some evenings he went to the Queen's Park Savannah and looked at football and after the match he walked across to Belmont where he was staying at his sister. It always struck him how people hurried, even after a football match. After some time he became accustomed to seeing them hurrying; after some time he was also hurrying. To what?

Some Saturday nights he went to dance with the tesses from the lane – and after the dance they all went to five o'clock mass in the nearest Roman Catholic church. One time he fell asleep during mass and when he awoke the church was empty, and when he got up and hurried outside he met the tesses drinking coconut-water and killing themselves with laughter.

Some nights he went out in the lane and talked with the tesses by the corner, cutting jokes and lying about women they never had. That was the life. And Monday morning he went to work.

There was that Monday morning with Mr Purcell, the chief clerk, and Mano, the office messenger. Mano had been absent since the Thursday, and that Monday morning, Mr Purcell met him in the outer office and looked at him through his thick-lensed spectacles.

'Mano,' Mr Purcell said.

'Yes, sah.'

Mano was a tall, loose-jointed Negro and he was bald all down the middle of his head and his hair was grey for he was getting old. 'Yes, sah,' he answered quickly.

'What do you have to say? Three days!' Mr Purcell held up three fingers. 'What do you have to say?'

'Sah.' Mano lifted a hand as if it didn't belong to him and he didn't look at Mr Purcell.

'I'm too soft with yuh-awl. Too soft!' Mr Purcell said.

'My lady, sah,' Mano said softly.

Mr Purcell leaned forward and cocked his head to one side. 'Your what?'

'My lady, sah.'

'Always with the same lame excuse. Look! If you people don't want to work – very well! But when you absent yourself like this you keep back a whole set of people.'

Mano said, 'All right, sah. But my lady –'

'Look, I don't want to hear excuses. I am tired of excuses.'

Mano stood looking at Mr Purcell, without any words to his tongue.

'What's wrong? Look! There are some things to be taken down to Boyle's. Hurry and get them off.'

'All right, sah. All right, sah.'

Afterwards, when he went outside, he met Mano near the toolshed in the yard, sitting on a box. There were big tears in Mano's eyes.

'What happen, Mano?'

'You been working here for some time,' Mano said. 'You come an' meet me here. You think I's a lazy man?'

'No, Mano.'

'Tell me the truth, Mr Castle. You think I's a lazy man?'

'No, Mano.'

'All right. But you know what the boss, Mr Purcell, think? He think I's a lazy man.'

'If he say so, Mano, he making joke.'

'Was no joke. He was serious. Tell me how I only bringing lame excuse. Tell me that right there in the office this mornin'.'

'Mr Purcell's crazy. You's not a lazy man, Mano.'

'You know it ent good when you workin' a place for a boss to think you lazy. It ent good. They does want to spite you. An' I's a man with nine chillren. It ent good.'

'You's not a lazy man, Mano.'

'Thursday evenin' I went home an' get a message how the wife sick up Manzanilla by she sister. I had was to run up there quick-quick. No time to send message. Everything topsy-turvy. The woman dying. Rush she to hospital. See 'bout the chillren. Nobody to see 'bout the chillren. All kinda worries.'

'And you didn't tell that to Mr Purcell?'

'When I open me mouth to tell him, he saying somethin'. He is boss.'

'You shoulda told him.'

'No chance. He didn't give me no chance to talk.'

'You shoulda told him. Just say, excuse me, sir. Just say that and then tell him.'

'He woulda think I lying.'

'He couldn't think that.'

'Yes, man. You don't know these people. I's not human like them. They's human but you's a machine far as they concern. Can't fight them. I's an old man. Wuck hard to get. Nine o' them I have, not three or four. Nine! Is only one time a poor man have a chance in the world an' that's when he young an' he don't know an' he don't begin to care. After that he begin to walk on a straight line like a damn soldier, he's nutten… I's a poor man an' I old, but praise God ev'rybody have to dead. Big an' little, rich an' poor.

Praise God ev'rybody have to dead, because it will be like hell for a man to see trouble without end.'

He left Mano sitting there on the box near the toolshed and tears were in his eyes and grief was messing up his voice. He remembers that.

Before he was married, Walter remembers how, at the end of the fortnight, when he got his salary he would go with the other fellows from the office down at Jackie's and punch tunes in the jukebox and eat fried chicken and drink rum or beer and talk, talk. Talk about women, talk about politics, talk about the job, about the world, talk in liquor-twisted voices, and sometimes, afterwards, they would go down by Cicada nightclub or out on The Strip. Monday morning you came to work and the fellows said, 'That was a good time we had last night, eh!' What was a good time? he would think. How the hell was that a good time? You sat there half drunk between cigarette-smoke and you ate fried chicken and you cracked the bone and sometimes the marrow ran down the side of your mouth and fell on to the front of your shirt and you had to wipe it off and listen to obscene jokes, or sometimes a woman with a big backside passed before the door and somebody pointed at her and everybody looked and then gave their opinion: what they would like to do with her and where and how. And then at the nightclub you'd drink rum and dance with a whore with bulging breasts and a short, tight-fitting silken dress, and perhaps you'd go to her room somewhere on some alley street, or you'd remain there and talk yourself to boredom, and drink the rum and watch the aimless curl of cigarette-smoke in the dimly lit room. That was a hell of a good time! Yes, sir. That was a good time!

What is a good time?

Now he remembers the night there at the party at Centeno. Parris from the office had invited Carlton and him, and there was a girl named Cicely to whom Parris introduced them. He had worn, for the first time, a new pair of shoes which pinched his toes, so he didn't dance; and the girl, Cicely, came over to where he was sitting and began speaking. He remembers how she smiled that time, with her teeth and her eyes and her lips, and how beautiful she was, and how he asked her to dance, and how they danced despite the pinching in his toes. He danced only one dance and then sat down and told her about his new shoes and how they were pinching his toes, and she laughed and said that she would keep it a secret from the others.

That was a good time. And when the party was over, he took her home. Carlton had a car and Cicely and he sat in the back seat. That night he didn't kiss her, he made a date for the movies the following evening. That night and all of the following day he prayed for evening, and when it came, he called for her and she came out in a white dress with red roses printed at the hem and on the sleeves. He remembers that, and how good he felt walking into the cinema with her, and how during the movie he touched her hands there in the semi-darkness, and how slender her fingers were and warm and how his heart beat within his chest, and after, when he was taking her home, she leaned on his arm and there were things like spears sliding up and down his chest and something cold dripping down to the pit of his stomach, and how it was, the touch of their lips, as he said goodnight, and how large were her eyes when she turned them up to look at him.

All of the following day he thought of her, and the day after that he thought of her, and that same evening he visited her at home. She didn't care to go to the movies, so they walked around the Savannah and sat on one of the benches; and he was content just to be near to her, knowing that she was right next to him, and for a long time they found no words to speak.

'I think of you every moment,' he said.

She looked at him. 'You shouldn't,' she said.

'And why not?'

'You shouldn't. Really.'

'I like your company,' he said.

'I enjoy your company too.' Her voice was kind and apologetic. 'Do you have many girlfriends?' she asked. 'Tell me of yourself.'

So he sat there, with the stars above his head and the spears sliding in his heart, and told her about himself.

'You don't love me?' she asked suddenly, hopefully.

'Why you ask?'

'Because I don't want to… It wouldn't make sense… You shouldn't.'

'Why?'

'Because… I'm going away.'

'Where to?'

'America. My uncle is sending for me.'

'That's nice,' he said. 'It should be exciting.'

'It should be,' she said. 'You're glad that I am going?'

'Would it make a difference if I am?'

'Is it important that things always make a difference?'

'I don't know for sure what is important. Do you?'

'Well, feeling. I think how you feel is important.'

'Whether that changes things or not?'

'Well, if you put it that way – yes.'

'And you still want to know if I'm glad you're going?'

'Well, I did ask you.'

'Okay. I'm not glad. Don't ask me why.'

She pressed her hand into his. Cars cruised by with park lights on; couples passed on the pavement, walking slowly, sometimes silent, sometimes speaking in low tones.

'When? When are you…?'

'Next week,' she said. 'I should have told you. I wanted to tell you the last time we were together but I was afraid.'

'Afraid?'

'That you would have stayed away. Now I guess… well…'

'Do you want to go?' he asked.

'Oh, I was all excited about it for months and months. Everything here seemed so dull and pointless. I was only waiting-waiting… I guess it was I… You know? I used to sit and expect things to happen – you know – like you read in books, and nothing ever happened, of course. The strange thing is that when I was certain that I would be going, I said I'd take a little fling at enjoying myself; I'd do things I was always afraid of doing, not bad things, I mean adventurous things, like talking to a boy first, like with you, laughing, dancing. And you know what? I enjoyed it. For the first time, I began to enjoy myself. I never imagined that I could have enjoyed myself so. Funny, life began to mean something that time. Then I met you.'

'And meeting me changed nothing?'

She raised her head that time, registering in her large eyes objection to the question.

'Sorry,' he said. 'I mean, do you still have to go?'

'I have to go. Mama… And you know, Uncle's expecting me.'

'I see,' he said rather sadly.

'You are sorry that I'm leaving?'

'Yes.'

'And I'm sorry too. Why did we have to meet at such a time?'

'I don't know… Next week, by plane?'

'Yes, by plane. Just a few hours and…'

'… and you'll be in New York.'

'You know, there's a funny feeling inside of me when I'm with you. Do you feel anything strange?'

'Something like spears sliding, and like something cold dripping?'

'Yes. I feel something so strange.'

They fell silent.

'It wouldn't be sensible,' she said. 'We would only hurt ourselves.'

He thought a while, then said, 'Maybe we've already hurt… I mean, you want me not to see you again?'

'Oh no. It's all right. I mean, I want to continue seeing you as long as I can, but that mightn't be so smart, you know.'

'Let's walk,' he said. 'I feel to stretch my legs.'

'All right.'

So they walked over near by the botanical gardens, their hands swinging, touching.

He remembers that time, and how afterwards, when they were going home, how silent they were and how he took her in his arms there in the shadows near her house, and how tender she was and what a thrill it was kissing her, feeling her go limp until she came alive and pushed him away, panting.

He saw her three times during the following week. The day before she left, they agreed that he would not come to the airport to see her off, but the night when she was leaving he went up to Piarco with Carlton and stood in the crowd and watched her board the aeroplane. And the day after, a feeling of

146

loneliness and loss came over him and he sat all day, thinking of her.

That was the same day that Mano came into the office, his face deeply lined with grief, and told them that his wife was dead. The office staff made a collection to purchase a wreath for the funeral, and the boss, Mr Purcell, told Mano that he was very sorry and gave him the remainder of the day off from work.

The same evening Parris and he went down by Jackie's and drank beer, and all that time he was thinking of Cicely and reproaching himself for being a coward at allowing her to leave when he wanted her so, and he was all cut up inside and angry with himself, and he told Parris and Parris said that that was how the world was.

'You have to take what you want, boy. Nobody give you anything. You get what you want, how you could. But this is a lesson. Life is a series of lessons; by the time you learn them all, it doesn't matter. I guess a man has to be lucky and make the favourable mistakes in life. You must make mistakes; only luck will save you.'

That time they were sitting there at Jackie's, sipping beer and talking, Saga appeared out of nowhere in a coloured shirt with crazy patterns, his hair slicked back, flashing a smile of gold.

'Walter! Walter! It's you, man,' Saga called, shoving his way towards him. And he stood and greeted Saga and introduced Parris to him, offered him a seat and called for another beer for Saga.

'Wait! Lemme look at you! Jesu! Man! Boy! I've been hoping to run into you. I lost the address you gave me. Remember?'

'Well, how are you? Heard you went away to the States or somewhere.'

'Yes. Spend two years. Left in a hurry, couldn't make it to see you.'

'Well, how was it?'

'Good. Good. Lotta work. Lotta fun too. Women. Yes, man! You get to know lots of people, man; get to feeling like you's somebody in the world after all.'

And Saga told him how it had been in the United States and how he had met some Trinidadians and other West Indians up there at New York, and what parties they had, and what women and liquor.

'Boy, I'm real glad for you,' Walter said. 'What about Evangeline?'

'You wouldn't believe it. We got married.'

'No!'

'Yes. After I got to New York you know we used to correspond and I wanted somebody to help me handle my business. Well, I sent for her. We even have a kid. Boy, that woman is big as a salt-beef barrel. Every day she tell me she's on diet and every day she gets bigger. Must be the family. You know she comes from a big breed of people. You should see her brother – six-foot-three and nearly three hundred pounds! What about you? Married yet?'

'Not yet.'

'Good. Boy, I must see you sometime to really talk. Must invite you home.'

'Yes.'

'Yes.'

That time they sat and talked and drank until they were high with liquor, and Saga had to ring for a taxi to take them home.

Now Walter remembers how it was that time when he stopped all the drinking and whoring and went back to the library, back to books. Every night before he went to sleep he read, and some-times wrote down some of the things he wanted to remember in a notebook. Long into the night he would sit reading, and Ruth, his sister, noticing lights on in his room, would call out, 'Walter! You there, Walter?'

'Yes.' He was there reading elementary psychology or the Greek philosophers or a novel by Zola or some poems out of the book of American verse. Yes, he was there and would be there a long time.

One night they were in the dining-room taking supper: Ruth, her husband Lester, and he.

Ruth said, 'Walter, you getting thin. Look at you!'

'You find so?' he asked.

'Don't you find he's getting thin, Lester? Like he's not eating.'

'A little thin, yes,' Lester said.

'Is this staying up nights, reading, reading,' Ruth said. 'This staying up isn't agreeing with you, boy. Look how thin you getting! What happen, you want to go mad or something? Sometimes I open my eyes from sleep and see lights on in your room and wonder if you there that late hour. Lester, you better tell him this setting up nights isn't good for him. You better advise him.'

'Walter,' Lester said. 'This setting up isn't good for your constitution, you know.'

'It's all right, don't worry,' he said.

'You always all right. I don't want you to get sick or go mad or something. You losing too much night rest. That isn't good.'

'All right, Ruth, don't worry so much,' he told her.

'I have to worry. If I don't worry, who will worry? Somebody have to worry. If you was married now, your wife would do the worrying. Why don't you get married? Eh? What you afraid of? Marriage is a good thing. Lester, tell him that marriage is a good thing.'

'Walter, marriage is a good thing,' Lester said.

'I mean, Lester, advise him. You're a man and he might understand you better.'

'Walter, marriage is a very good thing for a young man. You should try it,' Lester said.

'You really mean that, Lester?'

'I really mean that,' Lester said.

'You better tell him. If I tell him he will think it's joke I'm making,' Ruth said. She got up and cleared the table and left the two of them.

Lester laughed and said, 'Your sister's worried.'

'She shouldn't be.'

'But you go ahead and learn from books while you still think it's important.'

'What you mean?'

'I read some books myself. But there comes a time when a man realizes that it's not as important as he used to think. He realizes that living life is far more important than observing it or reading about it.'

'Well, I've done some living,' Walter said. 'But I don't know where I'm going. I just find myself moving with the crowd, being

pushed by them, being pushed with them. I don't know where I
am.'

'So you try to find out by reading those books?' Lester asked.

'I expect the books to help,' he said.

'I remember some words by Walt Whitman:

> "You are also asking me questions, and I hear you,
> I answer that I cannot answer, you must find out for
>   yourself."'

'I understand,' he said.

'You understand,' Lester said. Good. A word is sufficient for
the wise.'

9

'What time is it?' the man asks.

'Oh!' the woman exclaims, startled. 'I thought you were asleep.' She had stolen into the room softly, fearing to awaken him.

'What time is it?'

'Ten to two,' she answers.

'Ten to two,' the man says, opening his eyes. 'It's a long day.'

'Because you're resting. Sunday always appears to be the shortest day to me, guess it's because it's supposed to be a rest-day.' She stands, waiting for him to comment, but the man says nothing.

'Well, I'd better wake the baby and give her her feed, then take a rest myself. I'm tired.' She turns around and heads for the door. 'Do you notice anything strange?' she asks, at the doorway.

'No. Why?'

'Don't you miss Mr Sylvestre?'

'He!'

'Doesn't look like he'll come today,' she says.

'Look, if he comes tell him I'm sleeping.'

'All right.'

'Wait. If he comes, better wake me if I'm sleeping.'

'All right. I'll do that.'

'…I can't sleep anyway.'

'Is it I? Did I wake you?'

What the hell are you apologizing for? the man thinks. 'You didn't wake me,' he says. 'I can't sleep, that's all. I just keep thinking.'

'Thinking?'

'Yes, thinking. Sometimes Sylvestre is such a nuisance, but this afternoon I'll talk to him. I feel like talking to him.'

'I hope you don't argue. You all argue so much,' the woman says.

'You'd better wake the child and feed her,' the man says, sitting upright in bed now and preparing to get out. 'Think I'll go into the living-room… No. Think I'd better take a bath. Yes, I'd better bath.'

'There's a clean towel on the rack, but water, I don't know if there's any water in the pipes.'

'Damn it!'

'If you want to bath, you'd better hurry. The water goes off anytime on Sunday.' The woman turns and leaves the room. The man prepares to leave for the bathroom.

He hears her in the adjoining room. 'Shh, Cherrie! Come, darling! Hush. Come, sweetheart, and take your feed.'

He hears the child sighing and making protesting noises as she's awakened.

There is water in the pipes. The man bathes quickly, rubbing his skin vigorously and splashing about under the shower. He soaps his skin once, rinses it, soaps it again, rinses it and is done. He dries his skin slowly before he leaves the bathroom. In the bedroom he changes into clean clothes, combs his hair, then he goes into the living-room, seats himself and is about to reach for the newspapers when Mr Sylvestre enters.

'Good evening to you, Brother Castle,' Mr Sylvestre says.

'Good evenin', Mr Sylvestre. Take a seat.'

'Thank you, Brother.' Mr Sylvestre lowers himself into the nearest chair. He is a short, bow-legged man with a black, round, smooth face with large, round eyes. He looks like a salesman who has been unsuccessful all day and is quite close to admitting himself beaten, but is holding on with grim determination. His tone is underpitched and there is an apologetic ring to it, as if he is accustomed to being humbled.

'How is the family?'

'Family's well, thanks.'

'Hope I haven't disturbed you.' There is appeal and humility in his eyes. 'You were reading the newspapers?'

'Well, not exactly. Had a hard morning?'

'Brother Castle, I don't know what this world is coming to. I don't know.' There is a sadness in his voice. 'The people are gone; gone away from the Lord. Gone away, taken away, and when the Lord would enter, when He comes knocking on their doors, they shut them against Him.'

Walter does not speak.

'But, Brother, it is written: "All these things and more shall come to pass." ' He unzips his briefcase and takes out a Bible. 'It is written here. If you turn to the prophet Isaiah, chapter one, verse three, you will read' – he turns the pages of the Bible – ' "The ox knoweth his owner and the ass his master's crib; but Israel doth not know, my people doth not consider." That is what Isaiah says. Sad, but true. You do not believe me? Look around you. The jails are filled, there is anger and wickedness upon the face of the earth. Look in your newspapers – stories of rape and robbery and murder! What have we done with God's earth? We have made it a gambling-house and a battlefield. There is no meaning to life. People are lost. They do not know where to turn. Money is a disease and poverty a curse. Why?' Mr Sylvestre pauses.

Walter looks at him without speaking.

'Why, Brother, why?' It is as if he is speaking to a congregation, a congregation that is not there. 'We have listened to the call of Babylon too long. We have allowed the Tempter to come in amongst us and to be victorious over us. We do not remember that we have to answer to Someone much greater than ourselves. We are heavy with sin, and some of us even deny the existence – the existence, Brother – of Almighty God.' And now, his voice is slow and heavy as if it is bearing the burdens of the world. 'Let us turn to the Bible.' His voice is soft now. 'Isaiah, chapter twenty-four, verse twenty, says: "The earth shall reel to and fro like a drunkard, and shall be removed like a cottage; and the transgressions thereof shall be heavy upon it; and it shall fall and not rise again…" And have we not fallen? Are we not like drunk men in a dark gutter? Are we not now in a pit? And how shall we rise unless the Lord takes compassion on us? Listen to Isaiah: "We grope for the wall like the blind, and we grope as if we had no eyes: we stumble at noonday as in night; we are in desolate places as dead men." Isaiah tells us that we are already in the darkness. We are in the darkness because we fail to recognize God. We have taken hold of Babylon. We are without faith. We have no God. So we stumble at noonday as in night…'

'Perhaps it's not easy to believe,' Walter says. 'Simply saying "I believe" does not mean that one really believes.'

'Perhaps you are confusing belief with understanding, Brother.'

'Belief must be based on something, I think,' Walter says. 'Knowledge is the basis of belief. If a man does not know, does not understand, how can he believe?'

'Faith, Brother. Faith is the basis of belief in God, not knowledge.'

'There has to be a basis for your faith.'

'If a man trusts God and asks him for help, that man will be helped,' Mr Sylvestre says. 'But he must trust God.'

'That is not reasonable, Mr Sylvestre. How can you expect a man to appeal to a God in which he might not believe, to prove the existence of that very God to which you ask him to appeal?'

'You do not prove,' Mr Sylvestre said. 'You do not understand, Brother. Don't you believe in God, Brother Castle?'

Walter is silent now.

'Don't you believe, Brother?' There is alarm and distress in Mr Sylvestre's voice.

'Which God?'

'What do you mean, Brother? Which God?'

'I mean, which God?'

'The God of the Holy Bible. The God that created the heavens and the earth and made man – '

'The God that allowed Satan to tempt Adam, knowing – because God knows and sees all things – knowing that Adam was no match for Satan?' Walter asks.

'Brother, Brother! Adam had free will. Man has free will.'

'But Adam could not stand up to Satan. Satan was too powerful. Satan had influenced one-third of the angels in heaven. How could a mere man stand against him?'

'God had two-thirds of the angels. By your own argument you admit that God is more powerful than Satan. Why did Adam not choose to obey God? We are too small to understand the mysteries of God. In time, Satan will be destroyed.'

'I don't know,' Walter says. 'What I don't understand is that we are still given a storybook God in what is supposed to be an age of enlightenment. A man wants to believe, but it is difficult for him to reconcile what he experiences, what he sees every day, with a God such as the one you speak of.'

'God is the great Mystery,' Mr Sylvestre says.

'I agree with you.'

'"Because thou hast forgotten the God of thy salvation and hast not been mindful of the rock of thy strength, therefore shalt thou plant pleasant plants and shall set it with strange slips." Isaiah seventeen, ten. Your science has discovered much and is still engaged in discovering, but in the midst of it all there is doubting and uncertainty. The world is a warring sea lost in the noises of its own turmoil. You cannot believe because you want proofs and reasons; you cannot believe because you find it difficult to imagine someone greater than yourself. What is man? A moment, a few years, a sigh and death? What is man? I tell you, Brother, unless you seek the Lord now, find Him and accept Him, you are heading for destruction. The time is coming, the moment is near; the longer you resist Him, the harder it will be.'

'Mr Sylvestre, you are the man of God; what are you doing to save the world that you are so certain needs saving?'

'I am preaching the Word. And there are others like me, carrying the Word to the four corners of the earth. Once we have done that, our work is done,' Mr Sylvestre says, with a sense of actual achievement.

'What Word do you carry? Your God is oversimplified, you deny a man the right to question or to doubt. Believe or go to hell, you say. As simple as that! All men want to believe in another life or something, and because we want to believe, in spite of all that appears reasonable, we will stretch our hands to a dream that has no reasonable basis.'

'Brother,' Mr Sylvestre says in a kindly voice, 'I am sorry for you.'

'Yes?' Walter asks.

'Yes, Brother. For what a man seeks that shall he find; and if you choose to seek not God, but reasons, you will find, not God, but reasons; and the fire of hell will be waiting,' Mr Sylvestre says in the same kindly voice.

'You talk only of a God of vengeance. What about a God of love?'

' "I form the light and create darkness," ' Mr Sylvestre intones. ' "I make peace and create evil: I the Lord do all these things." Isaiah forty-five, seven. God is God and He has his reasons. Obscure as they might seem to you, He has reasons for allowing to be done all that is done. We cannot hope to understand. That is why I say believe and be saved.'

'Believe…'

'What is important, Brother, is not the explanation of God or of a god, not the fact of that god's reality, but the belief in such a god. For without belief in something greater than himself, a man is very little more than another animal.'

'Mr Sylvestre, even if I agree with that part about belief in something greater than yourself, that does not make God any more real than he is,' Walter says.

' "I am the first and I am the last; and beside me there is no God." Isaiah forty-four, six. That is sufficient proof for me. But listen, Brother: let us assume that there is no God, that He doesn't exist; and let us say that we manage to explain one and we have you believing in his existence; then, Brother, you have something to be guided by, you have someone to look up to.'

'I understand that, but that does not alter the real situation,' Walter says.

'But wait,' Mr Sylvestre says. 'Wait. Let us reverse the situation. Let us say that there is God, that God actually is and that we are not able to explain his existence, we are incapable of proving that he exists; to you, then you have nothing. Then, what a calamity for us all! You see, Brother?'

'I see, Mr Sylvestre.'

'You look for signs and wonders and these signs appear before your eyes, but you do not see. It is written: "Behold, a virgin shall conceive and bear a son and shall call his name Immanuel." That is the greatest sign. That is the sign we must observe.'

'It is easier for you, Mr Sylvestre. Easier.'

'Perhaps, Brother Castle.'

'I look for a God of this world, I look for God to come into Webber Street and down George Street and up Laventille. I look for God, or for the power of God, or for the men of God, to do something about the poverty and the oppression and the crime in the world. When I do not see an end to these things, when I see them continuing and getting worse, I ask, where is God? I ask, is God not of this world, is God a God of the Bible and of the dead, or God of the rich and not of the poor, and in some parts, God of the white and not of the black? You do not know how difficult it is, Mr Sylvestre. It is easy to say believe – quite easy. But when you are here, living next door to hooligans and prostitutes, when the girl next door is raped and the boy next door is charged for robbery and the woman next door commits suicide, you know that God is not here, that He was never here. Look at the amount of churches in Port of Spain! Look at the amount of masses that are sung, and the amount of gospels read! But look at this city and ask, really ask yourself, if there is anything or anyone like God in it, and you must answer no, there is no God here. If he was here, he has left. And I hear it is so all over the world.'

Mr Sylvestre has much to say; it is there on his smooth black face; it is there in his eyes. But his lips tremble.

'You understand me, Mr Sylvestre?' Walter says.

Mr Sylvestre moistens his upper lip with the tip of his tongue. 'I am trying to understand you, Brother Castle,' he says. 'Let me tell you. "God is not the God of the dead but of the living." Matthew twenty-two, thirty-two.'

'He is not?'

'He is not of the dead, Brother. But you must realize that He made a world and He put men in it to live. These men must make their contribution. We see the problems that confront us, we see the dangers in our midst, and we expect someone else to solve them. That is not reasonable. That is not fair. You, Brother Castle; what have you done about all these things which you say are wrong?'

'What can I do, Mr Sylvestre,' Walter says quickly.

'That is just the problem. You ask what you can do. Everyone can do something. You doubt God's existence and yet you expect Him to solve your problems. Even if He solves them, you wouldn't know it is He because you do not accept Him, and therefore do not know how mysterious are His ways. God is prepared to intervene, but man must solve his own problems,' Mr Sylvestre says.

'What chapter of the Bible you get that out of, Mr Sylvestre?'

'That's not in the Bible, but that is my opinion.'

'I see.'

' "Seek and ye shall find; knock and it shall be opened unto you." That is in the Bible, Brother.'

'I know.'

'Well, Brother, you seek, and you shall find a way to make your contribution, to do something to solve the problems that you see. This is my way. And now, Brother Castle,' Mr Sylvestre says, straightening himself in the chair and reaching into his briefcase, 'I have some books here for you. They are very valuable and will be of great assistance to you in your search for God.'

Walter listens. He knows it would have come to this. Mr Sylvestre had to peddle his magazines and stuff.

'This one here,' Mr Sylvestre says, holding up a thin magazine with a green cover, 'this one explains prophecies and is written by eminent scholars of the church. Want to have a look at it?'

'I don't think so, Mr Sylvestre.'

'Very well. This one is just the book for people who doubt. It is one of the most powerful books, giving arguments for and against God's existence and proving beyond the shadow of a doubt that God does in fact exist. You will take it?'

'Well…'

'Only seventy-five cents, this one,' Mr Sylvestre says, waving another magazine at Walter. 'Despite its small size, it contains answers to the most baffling of scriptural questions. This?'

'I have read many books, Mr Sylvestre.'

'All right. Do you have a copy of the Holy Bible?'

'I don't have one.'

'Good. I have a lovely copy here and I am certain that you would like to have it. If you don't want this,' he says, taking the Bible from the briefcase, 'then I have a better bound copy at home, I can bring it around for you.'

'I will take this one, Mr Sylvestre, but at the moment –'

'I understand. All right. I will leave it here with you and you will tell me when I should pass back, but that won't be necessary,

I pass by here every Sunday. So you will… I mean, we will see about that. Well, Brother, it is good to talk to people like you, and I am certain that the Lord will show you the light. A man like you cannot remain much longer in the darkness.' Mr Sylvestre rises. 'I think I will leave you now.'

Walter also rises. Mr Sylvestre puts out his right hand; Walter takes it; they shake hands.

'Good afternoon, Mr Sylvestre.'

'Good day, Brother Castle, and say good day to the Sister Castle for me.'

'All right, Mr Sylvestre.'

'All right, Brother.'

Walter walks to the door with Mr Sylvestre, and after the man walks through the doorway, he shuts the door after him. Now he turns and moves towards the bedroom. Sprawled in soft slumber is his wife, and lying across her breasts, also asleep, is their daughter. Walter stands and looks at them and something soft and slow moves within him, and in his mind he begins to go back to times past.

10

Now Walter remembers that carnival time. It was the first time that he saw Stephanie. She came with two of Lester's cousins whom Ruth had invited down from Arouca to spend carnival in Port of Spain. Carnival Saturday night he came home and met them getting ready to go to dance. As soon as he saw her he became sorry that he had promised to take out the Barbadian girl from next door, who had come to Trinidad for carnival. But they all went to the same dance, and when he met Alford, a fellow from the office, at the dance, he steered Alford at the Barbadian girl and concentrated on Stephanie. And all that night they had a good time, and Sunday morning, after dance, he took her home, and she was resting her head on his shoulder in the taxi, going home.

Then Sunday night – how could he forget that? Alford came to meet the Barbadian girl and again they all went to the same dance. The girls wore jeans and crazy carnival shirts and sailor caps, and he had a flask of rum in the hip-pocket of his jeans. That was another good night, and Monday morning after dance they all walked down Charlotte Street, down to the headquarters of Trinidad All Stars steel-band and sat around on the pavement, half-asleep and tired, and waited for the steel-band to get on the street, and when the steel-band, Trinidad All Stars with Jitterburg holding the flag, came on the street, people got off the pavements and moved from where they were leaning, resting, and jumped into the band, with everyone having his partner. That time, all of them, the Barbadian girl and Stephanie and Lester's two cousins and another fellow and he, held on to each other and formed a line and jumped into the band. That was a time! All down Charlotte Street and then across Queen Street and down Frederick Street they went, dancing to the rhythm of the steel-band, and Stephanie was smiling as if she had never had such a good time. Yes, and the sun mounted in the sky and he had to get to work, but first he wanted to listen to the clash between Trinidad All Stars and Invaders, the big band from Woodbrook. For when Trinidad All Stars was going back down Charlotte Street, the wire came that Invaders steel-band was coming across Duke Street. Then the two bands met right at the corner of Duke and Charlotte Streets. Invaders played well, they played fine, but they couldn't beat Trinidad All Stars. He stood with his arms encircling Stephanie and just listened to the music the steel drums made, and then he was satisfied and left Stephanie and the others and Alford and he went to work.

That was the same morning they met Briggs about a block away from the office, sitting on the pavement, too tired to make another step, and between Alford and he, they carried Briggs to work. That was the same morning too that Mr Purcell came to work wearing a sailor cap and there was lipstick all over his face and he didn't realize what the staff was laughing at. And that time too, as soon as Miss Regis came in she fell asleep on her typewriter, and Santo came in drunk and wanted to kiss Mr Purcell. And all that morning, despite his tiredness, he kept thinking of Stephanie and praying for the morning to come to an end so that he could go and meet her. How could he forget that carnival? The bands appeared bigger, their colours more dazzling, the beat of the steel-bands more compelling. Everything was right. And when, on Tuesday night, they were jumping up in the street and he bent and kissed her, he could have cried because in a few hours' time it was going to be over.

But carnival was over, only carnival, not the relationship that had sprung up between Stephanie and him. Afterwards he visited her at her home at Arouca: sometimes they would take long walks in the cool nights, and sometimes they went to a movie. One moonlight night with the breeze sharp and the stars scattered all over the sky, they went for a walk. They hardly spoke many words, but that night was filled with violin music and there was love between the two people, and he held her hands and kissed her and afterwards asked her to be his wife, and she said yes, very quietly, and folded her hands around his, and they walked home without speaking another word; and they didn't make any plans or set any date or anything, they walked home, holding hands, and afterwards he wrote the letter asking her father's permission.

And shortly before he was married he met Andrew, his brother, downtown.

'What's happening, Walter?' Andrew greeted him.

And he stood and looked at his brother, the son of his mother, and saw that he was getting fatter around the jowls and stomach and thicker about the neck.

'I'm all right, Andrew.'

'We hardly see each other. Ma told me you're getting married.'

'Yes. I'm getting married.'

'That's why we hardly see you?'

'No.'

'Why? You're busy?'

And he wanted to answer, No, I'm not busy. It's just that I don't care to see you. But he didn't say that. He bent his head and said, 'Yes. I'm a little busy.'

It was an oppressively hot day and the streets were crowded and Andrew took out his handkerchief and mopped his forehead.

'Sun's hot today,' Andrew said. 'You'll take a beer?'

'All right,' he said, not wanting to show hesitation.

They went and sat in a beer shop and Andrew ordered two beers.

'You're a man now, Walter,' Andrew said, smiling shyly as if he was with a stranger whom he was afraid of displeasing.

'I guess so. Everybody grows up,' he said after a while.

There were three stripes on Andrew's sleeves that time.

'I see you've been promoted,' he said.

'Yes.' Andrew looked at the silver stripes on his left shoulder, and passed his fingers over them. 'Got these a few months ago,' he said. 'Worked hard like hell too, you know. Had to work damn hard. I don't have the brains that you have.'

'You're doing well, Andrew. Congratulations.'

Andrew looked at him.

'I mean it,' he said.

There was a long silence that time and they sipped their beers and a fellow came in and looked into the booth where they were seated and seeing Andrew, Sergeant Andrew in his uniform, seated there, he said, 'Excuse me,' and withdrew his head.

'Joker,' Andrew said.

'Yes. How's Ma, Andrew?'

'The old lady's half an' half – you know?'

'Yes,' he mumbled.

'The small ones growing fast. You know Carol's in fifth standard. She's brighter'n Chris. I spoke to her schoolmaster the other day. He said she has a good chance of winning a college exhibition. Brains! Imagine Carol going to college.'

'That will be fine,' he said.

'But I'm worried about Chris. He's a funny little fellow.'

'He's growing up, Andrew. Maybe it's just how he's growing up.'

'Maybe. But I'm still worried about him.'

'You'll take another beer, Andrew?'

'Thanks.'

He asked for two beers.

'I'm getting married too,' Andrew said.

'Well… Congratulations.'

'Thank you. I've waited a long time to find a wife.'

'Better late than never.'

'Yes,' Andrew said. 'Better late.'

There was a stretch of silence like before it rains, with the clouds piling and the birds flying to nest.

'I invited Carmen to the wedding. I haven't seen Ruth as yet, and I want you to come. Bring some friends.'

He picked up his beer and sipped it. 'You invited Carmen?' he asked.

'Yes,' Andrew said. 'I want the family to be there.'

'Carmen says she's going to come?'

'She didn't say exactly. But I'm kinda hoping that she'll come. If you see her, remind her.'

'Okay, but it's hardly likely that I'll see her.'

'It… it was a funny thing to do, eh?' Andrew said.

'Yes.'

'You remember it? You were small that time. You remember?'

'I remember.'

'Okay, but tell me. Let's see if it's the same thing I'm thinking of.'

'All right. It's about the time when you refused to go to Carmen's wedding although Pap wanted you to go.'

'Yes, you remember, Walter. And you were vexed that time?'

'Everybody was vexed.'

'I was wrong. I was foolish,' Andrew said.

He made no comment. Andrew began to speak in an apologetic tone.

'Each man begins with his own ideas about how things should be. They might be wrong, but they're his own ideas. You understand?'

'I think so.'

'But afterwards you learn.'

'What you learn, Andrew?'

'That you didn't make the world, for one thing. And for another that alone, a man don't feel good. People need people. A man needs a family, something to belong to, and… and that you don't change people, you change yourself. I learned a lot. I was pretty hard on you long time, eh? But you wouldn't believe it, it was myself I was being hard on. I was trying to make up for something.'

'You made up for it?'

'There're some things a man can't make up for, some things he must accept. In a way, acceptance is as good as making up. Better, Walter.'

'Yes, Andrew.'

'I know I was hell to get on with, Walter.'

'Yes, Andrew.'

'Walter, we have to rebuild the family. Specially for Chris and Carol.'

'It will be hard to do at this time. Everybody's scattered. You're getting married and I'm getting married. It will be hard to do.'

'I know. But we can try. It's important. When a man doesn't belong, when he has to fight alone, achievements don't mean a thing. I don't mind saying this to you, Walter. I know you've been alone too.'

'Yes, Andrew, I've been alone for a long time.'

'A man gets to thinking a funny way when he's alone.'

'Yes. He knows that he has to fight the world.'

'You learnt that too?'

'Yes, Andrew, I learnt that. It's going to be hard to rebuild the family.'

'How does a man say he's sorry, Walter?'

'He doesn't say it.'

'No, I mean if a man's sorry and he wants to say it, how does he?'

'I don't know how.'

'I'm... Well, I'm sorry.'

'Sorry for what?'

'For not understanding. Especially for not understanding you.'

'It's all right, Andrew.'

'No, it isn't all right... But I'm sorry. You know something, Walter? You don't get back anything. You don't get back anything you lose... I mean, anything you let go.'

'Never?'

'Never.'

The silence came upon them that time; and still the noises were loud in the other parts of the building.

Andrew said, 'You'll take another beer, Walter?'

'That'll do,' he said.

'Okay, then let's go, boy.'

They walked out of the place, into the street which was still hot and crowded; and all that time he kept thinking of the family that was no more. And then he thought of the family that his brother was about to build, and of the one that he himself was about to build, and how Andrew had changed, and wondered what had changed him.

Now he thinks of the day he was married, how frightened he felt inside of him and how he kept grinning all the time so no one would suspect what was his true disposition. Yes, and after the wedding, Stephanie and he went to Mayaro for honeymoon. He remembers the wooden beach-house and the tall bow-bent

165

coconut trees, and the sight of the sea in the morning, and the sound of waves breaking on the shore whenever you awoke in the night, and the work-chants of fishermen pulling in seines on the beach, and the hush of the fishermen as the seine reached the beach, and the rush and scramble of vendors as they dashed in to fill their baskets with fish, and the leap of the fish tangled in the net, and the impassive faces of the fishermen as they saw that the seine had snagged seaweed, not fish, and the vendors began to walk away to where other fishermen were pulling another seine in; and how Stephanie and he sat with their legs in the water and looked out at the waves curling in to shore and listened to the roar of waves breaking and watched the silver spray and glistening white foam; and how they romped and tickled each other until one of them said surrender... And then the honeymoon was over.

He remembers the night when they moved into the apartment there on the third floor of the tenement building on Webber Street with their few pieces of furniture, and Mr Sears, Stephanie's father, was with them. They offered the truck-driver, who had helped them transport the furniture, a drink; and after he left, Walter sat there in the living-room and drank rum and talked with Stephanie's father, who remembered how it was the time when, as a young man, he had been married and had moved into a house with his wife; and while they were talking Stephanie kept pulling down the shutters and peeping downstairs and her father asked her whether she was afraid of the height, and she said she was not afraid and shut the window and closed the shutters and joined in the conversation; and after Stephanie's father left, how they sat right there in the living-room and clung to each other as if they were afraid of something.

And he remembers how it was, those first few months at the apartment; how he went home from work as soon as he knocked off and Stephanie, all fresh and clean and combed up, opened the door for him and they kissed and went into the bedroom and talked while he took his shoes and shirt off. And after supper they talked a while in the living-room, then she went in and called him and they lay on the bed and listened to the neighbour's radio, or romped and laughed and then fell asleep in each other's arms, leaving one small bulb lighting the room.

And he remembers the feeling of frustration when, after six months of marriage, he found that it was impossible to balance the budget. Bills, bills, bills. Where did so many bills come from? Yes. There were rent and light bills and furniture bills and grocery bills and instalments to be paid on the radio. And that night when he sat on the edge of the bed and smoked a cigarette and Stephanie lay at his side with her eyes open and neither of them speaking for a long time, then Stephanie reached out and touched him and said, 'I'd better get a job, Walter.'

'What?' he asked, as if he hadn't heard well.

'If I get a job I can help out with the bills. Maybe just for a while until we are able to bring things back in order. It wouldn't be hard on me. I can cook in the morning and we can take lunch to work. It wouldn't be hard on me.'

That was the time he was expecting promotion, and he reached out and took her face between his hands. 'No Stephanie,' he said. 'Not yet.'

'Why not, Walter? I can help. A wife is to help. And it won't be hard.'

'Let's wait a while, eh? Let's wait for a month.'

'All right,' she agreed, 'but it won't be hard on me.'

And he got into bed, but didn't go to sleep right away because he was thinking about the bills and hoping that he get the promotion and the increase in salary that went with it.

But two months passed and there was no promotion, and the bills mounted. Then he went home one evening and found Stephanie bristling with excitement.

'What's wrong, dear?' he asked. 'You look as if something is jumping under your skin.'

'I have something to tell you,' she said.

'All right. What is it?'

'Promise you won't be angry?'

'What is it?'

'It's nothing bad. Promise that you won't be angry?' She clung to his arm and looked up into his face. 'Promise?'

'All right. What's it?'

'Today I went to town,' she said.

'Is that all?' he asked, and sat down, half relieved.

'And,' she said, 'and I got a job. You're not angry?'

'Why should I be? Where'd you get this job?' He tried hard to sound casual.

'At the shirt factory. I was lucky. There were fifteen of us and they took on three. Don't you think I was lucky?'

'Yes, you were lucky.'

'They told me to come out tomorrow. And Walter, it won't be so hard on you now. And we can settle the outstanding bills.'

'Yes,' he said.

'You're not angry?'

'No.'

'So I can go to work tomorrow?'

'Yes.'

So his wife went out to work. And then, it was always hustling: breakfast to be prepared and lunch to be prepared, and the clock, the clock making haste, and the radio announcer saying, 'Ha, now if you have to get to work for eight, you're eight minutes late,' and so on, and so on. On an evening when he came home there was no nice clean freshened Stephanie to meet him at the door, no sir; that changed. She was as tired as he. Occasionally he reached home before she did.

One night he came in and met her preparing supper.

'I just came in,' she said. 'I worked late.'

'Do you have to work late?'

'Overtime. It's more money.'

'But do you have to?'

'I don't think so.'

'Then leave the overtime. I'm starving.'

'You're angry because supper isn't ready? But Walter, I just reached.'

'Okay. Okay. I'm going out.'

And he went out and came back drunk and puked on the floor and she had to pull off his shoes and clothes and help him to bed.

That was life: squabbling over bills and trying to make ends meet, and coming home tired and finding little comfort in a wife also tired. That was it. Then he met Annabelle.

'Walter,' Stephanie said, one evening, 'I've invited Annabelle and her husband here. Try to reach early from work tomorrow night.'

'Who's Annabelle?'

'A girl from the factory. The girl I'm always talking about. She's my good friend.'

'What's she coming for?'

'Just a visit. Tomorrow. Don't forget. Come home early.'

'All right.'

The following night he reached home early and Stephanie and he sat in the living-room waiting for the visitors. Annabelle arrived alone. She was a tall, attractive woman wearing a tight-fitting, knee-length skirt and her hair was tangled all over her head. She said she had misplaced the address and had knocked around a while before finding the correct one.

'Where's Tom?' Stephanie asked.

'Tom is somewhere. That man left home since evening and when he didn't come, I left. I left a note on the table for him. Honest, girl, I doesn't know what some men coming to these days. They leaves and goes out and drinks and gambles. It's a bitter shame.'

'Will you take a drink, Annabelle?' Stephanie asked.

'Thanks, sweetheart. I can do that.'

Stephanie got up and left for the drinks.

Annabelle looked at him and said, 'So you're Stephanie's wonderful husband.'

Walter smiled.

'She's always talking about you, you know.'

'And she's always talking about Annabelle.'

'But don't you go out? I mean, I've never seen you two at the dances the girls go to,' Annabelle said.

'Well…' Walter stalled.

Stephanie came back with the drinks.

'I was asking why you two don't come to the dances the girls go to,' Annabelle said.

'We go out,' Stephanie said.

'Where to?'

'Oh, the cinema sometimes,' Stephanie answered.

'The cinema! Sweet Christ, girl, so many nice dances and you go to the cinema! You-all are young. This is life. There's so little time, a boyfriend of mine used to say, and so little in it anyway, and so little of that little that we can get – you know, he was a college boy. Tom takes me dancing once a month. Child, this is life and I'm sixteen years young.' She laughed, showing her pink gums.

Stephanie smiled. 'Annabelle, you're a scream.'

'I just loves to have a time,' Annabelle said. 'What else to do? Work and kill yourself with worries about money? Not Annabelle!'

'You know they say I must join the union at the factory,' Stephanie said.

'Yes, sweetheart. You must join the union. I've been seven years in the union and sometimes we march. You know, sympathy marches for other places that are on strike. One day Mr Salim bring his freshness to one of the girls and when she didn't take him on, he fired her. Now, if that girl was in the union, Mr Salim couldn't touch her. You have to join. You have to belong to something. The workers must protect themselves because nobody protects the workers.'

'You really think it will make sense if I join, Annabelle?'

'But, sweetheart, that's what I'm telling you. You have to join. And I heard Mrs Brump, you know she's the shop-steward, say just now maybe we'll go on strike.'

'For what?' Stephanie asked.

'Wages, child. More wages. But that would mean that Mr Salim would want to get rid of some of the new girls. Thank God I has a husband. Maybe Tom likes to drink and gamble, but Tom's my husband and Mr Salim and the rest of them can very well excuse me if it comes to that. Sweetheart, you have to join the union. Anyhow, once they know you have a reliable man they don't bother you. But didn't I tell you about Pamela? Imagine the fastness of that woman asking me my age. I said, " Sweetheart, I'm not old and I can give any man a good time. Whaddu you want to know my age for?" That Pamela! Always in the same green skirt and pink blouse. Why don't she join the Birthday Club; we'll make her a present of a new suit of clothes. Asking me my age! The idea! By the way, you must join the Birthday Club. You know who's in it? Mrs Smart and Pinky and Mrs Martin and old Miss

Royal and that darling child that comes to work with her boy-friend every morning, Punella. I like Punella; she's so smart and up-to-date and she never wants to know my age. We work right next to each other and she tells me all about her boyfriends. The boy wants to marry her but his mother thinks he's too good for her. The old wretch – excuse me – wants a few drops of some-thing in her coffee on mornings. Don't you like Punella?'

'Punella?'

'Yes, the little, roundheaded girl with large, slanted eyes, and girl, she has a figure. Once we went to a party and that child looked sweet. She's right next to me and she always has a smile.'

'Oh, Punella!'

'Yes. The whole factory loves that girl. She's going to the dance too. Are you coming, Stephanie? You should come. Let your husband bring you. Tom is taking me if he's not too drunk, and that picky-head Elaine say she want to come. I can't understand Elaine. At her age she doesn't drink or smoke and she hasn't got a man. How the hell she lives God knows – excuse me, children; I think I'm in the factory. You coming to the dance?' she said, speaking at Stephanie and looking at Walter.

'I don't know,' Stephanie said, looking at Walter.

'If Stephanie wants to go, we can go,' he said.

'Of course Stephanie wants to go. It's next week Saturday and you'll have a good time. You know, after working at the factory whole week, you must have some sorta fun and excitement out of life, otherwise life means nothing and life must mean something even if it's just having a good time at a dance on Saturday nights and going home afterwards with your man hugging you up. Oh my, oh me. I've talked and talked. Look, I'd better leave now. I wanted to go to the cinema. Tom won't come again if he hasn't come as yet.'

'You going?' Stephanie asked.

'Yes. Tom will reach home and he wouldn't even see the note this hour because he must be drunk or something. Yes, I'd better leave now. I'll drop around and see you children some time.'

They saw Annabelle to the door.

'She's really a nice person,' Stephanie said after they had closed the door and Annabelle had gone down the steps.

'She's a hurricane,' he said.

'But she's very nice. You really want to go to the dance?'

'Well, we told Annabelle that we would be going, and I don't mind going.'

'All right then, we'll go. We can't study bills alone.'

That was settled. But on the very Saturday night of the dance, he came home hot with fever. Stephanie wasn't home. There was a note on the radio saying that she had gone to the hairdresser's and that his supper was in the oven and he could turn on the stove and warm it if it wasn't warm. That time he was roasting with fever and he didn't eat; he went and lay down and fell asleep and didn't know when Stephanie returned; but he found her, when he opened his eyes, leaning over him, and her hair was all nice and pressed swept up on the top of her head and her eyes were shining with excitement.

'What's wrong, Walter? You didn't eat. I left the food in the oven.'

'I have fever,' he said, drawing the covers over him.

She felt his neck and said, 'Yes. You have fever. You have roasting fever. How'd you get it?'

'I picked it up in the office and brought it home with me.'

'How you feeling?'

'Not good. Jesu, I can't go to the dance tonight. But you just cover me up and make me a cup of ginger tea and go ahead with the girls when they come.'

'You're crazy, Walter. I can't leave you here sick and go any place.'

'All I have's a little fever. Go ahead.'

'Well, I'm not going,' she said.

'I hope you don't think I picked up this fever for spite,' he said.

'Why'd you say that?'

'I don't know. It's just that we planned so much on going.'

'It's only a dance,' she said. 'There'll be others. You want anything to eat?'

'No. Just the tea.'

'All right, I'll go and make it.'

Later, after she had given him the tea, he was dropping off to sleep when he was awakened by a knocking on the door. It was Annabelle and the gang come to meet them.

'Oh Lawd! You children not ready yet,' he heard Annabelle say.

'We're not going again,' Stephanie told her.

'But why?'

'Walter – '

'Change his mind?'

'No. Sick.'

'Well, so help me!'

'He said I could go if I want, but – '

'Yes, I know, you can't leave the poor soul here alone. How'd he get fever?'

'Just got it.'

'Yes, just got it. Hell! Well, we're going. Tell that man to get better. Hell! It's a damn shame, though.'

He closed his eyes and pretended to be asleep when Stephanie came into the room right after, and crawled into bed beside him.

Annabelle came around fairly regularly; once or twice Tom came with her; and sometimes all of them went to the movies together. More than once he caught her looking at him out of the sides of her eyes. Then Annabelle ceased to visit them for a long period. He asked Stephanie if there was anything wrong between them. Stephanie said there was nothing that she knew of. Perhaps Annabelle just didn't feel like visiting them any more. He left it at that, but it didn't stay long at that.

One evening right after work he went up to Jerico by his mother. Carol, his little sister, had won a government college exhibition which was tenable in Port of Spain, so he had gone up to finalize arrangements by which she would come to Port of Spain and remain at his home, so she could go to college. As soon as he got out of the taxi, he saw Annabelle on the other side of the street. He went over to her.

'Hello, Annabelle,' he said. 'You're scarce as good gold.'

'Hello, Walter. I wanted to see you. I was going to come up at your office, but I was afraid what people would think.'

'But you don't have to worry about people, Annabelle; we're friends,' he said. 'You wanted to see me?'

'Yes, but you look busy now and what I have to say will take

173

some time. What about tomorrow, about this time? We'll go some place and talk,' she said.

'Something important?' he asked.

'Yes.'

'It's about Tom?'

'How'd you guess? It's about Tom and there's something else too. Can you make it tomorrow?'

'I can try.'

'I want you to be certain.'

'All right, look out for me. Where'll I meet you?'

'Right here, at this very time.'

'All right.'

'All right, Walter. And Walter,' she added, as he was about to leave, 'you don't have to tell anyone about this.'

On the following night, at the agreed time and place, he found himself waiting for Annabelle. He glimpsed her walking quickly towards him. When she realized that he had seen her, she walked more casually.

'Good night,' she said.

'Good night.'

'You come after all.'

'Didn't I tell you I'd come?'

'Sure. You're a man to your word. You tell Stephanie you came to meet me?'

'No.'

'Good. Let's go.'

'Where to?'

'Look. I'm a big woman and you're a grown man,' she said. 'I thought we'd go to a restaurant and have a bite and talk in the meantime.'

'I don't have money,' Walter said.

'It's all right. I have. You'll go to the restaurant?'

'Let's go. I'm always happy to have a little freeness,' he said, smiling.

They walked to a little place on Henry Street.

'Nice,' Annabelle said. 'Not much people here – I can take a drink. What about you?'

'I can use one.'

'Now tell me your problems, Annabelle,' he said, when the drinks had arrived.

'I'm a plain straightforward woman, Walter. I get in trouble because of that, but I can't change. I'm just cut out to be a straightforward person.'

'Whaddu you mean?'

'Well,' she said, sipping her drink first, then resting it before her, 'Tom is no use to me. Tom taken up with drinking and gambling. I'm a warm woman. A warm woman needs a man. Tom not that kinda man to me.'

'You want me to talk to him?'

'Talking wouldn't do no good.'

'Maybe if I talk to him he'll stay home more often. At least I can try. I don't like to see you so unhappy. I think I'll talk to Tom – that is, if you want me to.'

'Thanks for the offer, Walter. But talking won't do. Something wrong with Tom. And talking can't fix it. He's no use to a woman any more. You understand?'

Yes, he understood.

'I've tried to put up with it as long as I could bear it, but I'm not a cold woman. And I don't want to leave him.'

'You want me to advise you? Whaddu you want me to do?' he asked.

'You's somebody man, but you's a man, I can see that. Nobody have to tell me that.' Her fingers began to steal up along his arm. 'I know you're married. But you're… And I'm married too. I know it.'

And he knew. He knew and understood completely.

'You know,' Annabelle said, 'it's not really Tom fault. Tom had a hard-hard life. Tom was the second out of eleven children and he used to work on the cocoa estate in Sangre Grande before he run away and come to town and get work on the docks. Tom born in poverty and Tom get to be afraid of poverty. He always afraid that he don't have sufficient money. Tom work hard on the docks. Tom was a moneylender and he's a bitch where money is concerned. Is only since I married Tom that Tom eating good. He used to starve his belly just to have plenty money. Is only since I with Tom that Tom know how it is inside a cinema and about going to dance and races. Tom was a bitch with money and money do for Tom. Money dry up everything inside of him. Six years we married and every night it getting worse. Now we give up trying. Tom is a man without education, so he can't enjoy fine things like real rich people who's the same way he is. When that happen to a poor-class man it worse than when it happen to a rich man, because those people have culture and studies and things to help them, but poor Tom never even reach fourth standard, so what Tom have? Now he taken up with drinking and gambling like if gambling out his money would make him a man again. But I can't stand it. I can't stand it. Life is more than eating and wearing clothes and making joke with the girls in the factory. Life is more than a dance on Saturday night and having a party with the Birthday Club. I'm a woman with blood, and though I don't want to hurt Tom, I want a man who's a man to a woman, you understand, Walter?'

He understood. And he realized the significance of her fingers stealing along his upper arm, and her eyes, and her slightly parted lips revealing the edges of her teeth. Looking at her, he felt the blood flowing under his skin, and the warm blood sweeping up his loins.

'I didn't know things were so bad with Tom,' he said.

'It's not Tom they're bad with,' she said. 'It's me that's suffering.'

'I'm sorry,' he said.

'That's all you can say?'

'Well... I don't know.'

'I'm a straightforward woman and I likes a straightforward man. I know you're married. But that don't mean – '

'I love my wife, Annabelle.'

'Well I like that! You act as though I going to take you away from her. I know you love your wife.'

'You don't understand, Annabelle.'

'You'll take another drink? You'd better take one because I'm ordering a big one for myself.'

They downed their drinks hastily.

'You'll take me home?' she said.

'Where's Tom now?'

'I tell you Tom's only drinking and gambling all over the place. You'll take me home?'

'All right.'

'You not afraid?' she teased.

He smiled broadly.

'Of course you not afraid. You's a big man. You'll take me home?'

'All right, I'll take you home. Come, let's go.'

They walked to the taxi-stand. In the taxi she kept pressing against his side and he kept on talking to keep himself from thinking of the pressure of her body against his.

When they arrived at her home, she said, 'You won't come in for a while?'

'All right. For a while.'

The living-room was well furnished. He went over and stood looking at the huge radiogram and record-player.

She put on a Brook Benton record. 'Listen to that. I'll get you a drink. All right?'

And he stood there listening to the record and reading the back of the cover of a long-playing album. And when she came back with the drinks, wearing something thin, she stood and walked and did her best for him to take a good look at her.

'I don't think you want to stand whole night,' she said. 'Siddown.' She sat on the couch and indicated the seat at her side.

'Won't be staying long,' he said.

'I scare you so much?' she asked, and as he opened his mouth to protest, she smiled and said, 'You afraid I'll seduce you – that's the word, isn't it?'

'No. No. I'm not afraid.'

'Good. Well, siddown.'

So he sat and sipped at his drink and listened to the music. When the record was played out, he had finished his drink. He stood.

'I said I wouldn't be staying long,' he told her.

'You going already? You really afraid?'

He said nothing, and she stood and said, 'Take another drink. You can't leave on one leg. And, for Christsake, siddown. Nobody going to eat you.'

So he grinned and sat and she went and refilled the glasses.

'Walter,' she said, after she had returned and had seated herself next to him.

'Yes.'

'You prefer I call you Mr Castle?'

'Walter's all right.'

He sat waiting for her to say something. She said nothing. They drank in silence and he finished his drink and looked at her and got up, feeling as if he wasn't doing the right thing.

She stood and said, 'All right, I'm too old.'

'But you're not old, Annabelle.'

'Then…' she said, and held his arm, asking a question, and she was quite near to him, and her breath was on his neck – he could feel it, and he could feel the blood pounding across his temples and the excitement in his loins, and he put an arm around her and she led him into the bedroom where the lights were off. And afterwards he looked for his shoes, found them and put them on, and left without a word, and when he was a few feet off he heard her shutting the front door. That was the beginning. How had it really come about? What had he done to prevent it?

He never saw her again until one day she telephoned to ask him if he had forgotten her. He said he hadn't forgotten her. She invited him to her place. He said he would go. He went. Why did he go? He loved his wife. He didn't want to hurt her. Why did he go? And that wasn't all. He returned another time, and another. Beyond that time, he didn't return. That was the end. He remembers that time well.

'This is the last time, Annabelle,' he said. They were side by side on the bed, and the record-player was on in the living-room. The music was soft and the house almost entirely in darkness. His voice was low and even.

'Not yet,' she said, as if she didn't believe he meant what he had said.

'Now. This isn't good for either of us.'

'What will I do? And I love you.'

'This is bad. Wrong.'

'So many things wrong,' she said.

He turned, and she thought he was getting up to leave that time.

'Wait,' she said. 'Gimme a cigarette.'

And in the half light he felt for the cigarettes on the dresser, and lighted one and gave it to her. And when she was finished smoking the cigarette, he rolled over and got off the bed and put on his clothes, and she sat on the edge of the bed and watched him, and they didn't say a word, and he realized that she knew that he was serious, and leaving her that time he felt sad, and he didn't speak and neither did she. He left, and she never heard from him, and he never heard from her.

But one day, Tom, looking much older and harassed, came home and with a trembling voice and tears shining in his eyes, asked had they seen Annabelle.

'No,' Stephanie said. 'I can't remember when last Annabelle came here.'

'Four days I ain't seen Annabelle,' Tom said. 'Four days.'

'You searched?' Stephanie asked.

'Searched high and low. I was at San Fernando and when I came back, no Annabelle. Everything there in the house: furniture, radio, fridge, gram, everything, but Annabelle gone.'

Tom sat right there and cried, tears making his face look ugly and old. But they couldn't help him. They themselves didn't know anything about Annabelle. That was a hard thing.

Yes, and it was a hard thing too that evening a few months after when he went home after work and met Carol crying and Stephanie in pain. He remembers that time so well. He can actually see it.

There was Webber Street with a hush over it, and there on the pavements were policemen with riot helmets and riot staffs and service revolvers buckled down in holsters at their hips, and absent were the tesses who usually stood bunched talking on the pavement. Webber Street looked ugly with the garbage in mounds in the canal all down the length of the street, and looking ugly too was a woman bawling and wringing her hands while a policeman stood trying to calm her and two small children stood crying and clinging to her dress. 'My son! My son!' the woman wailed, and the small children clinging to her dress went 'Eh-h-h-h! eh-h-h-h eh-h-h-h!' like an alarm clock going off. The woman pitched herself to the ground, and another policeman came from across the street to help to lift her to her feet. Yes, and all around windows were shut and radios were on low.

'They chopped off her son hand in the riot,' somebody said.

'Chopped it off?'

'Yes, chop it off.'

That time he hurried across to where he lived and met Stephanie inside groaning in pain, and Mrs Walls, the woman who lived on the second floor, looking confused, and Carol like she wanted to cry.

'What's wrong?'

And they told him how fifteen members of a gang armed with cutlasses, knives, iron bolts and home-made guns had swooped down on Webber Street just a few minutes before, and how that time, Stephanie was going up the steps when she heard the explosions of guns and the screams of terror of the tesses caught off guard on the pavements, and how as she was running up the steps she stumbled and fell and Mrs Walls had to open her door and pull her inside. He had arrived just in time. They didn't know what to do.

'Best place is hospital,' Mrs Walls advised.

So they rushed her to the hospital, and afterwards he telephoned Ruth and told her what had happened; and she and Lester came down to the hospital and met him and he told them again what had happened, and they waited right there in the reception room with the smell of old phials and disinfectant for word about her condition.

They had put Stephanie in the maternity ward, the nurse said, but she said that the doctor was not allowing anyone to see the patient.

While they waited with a child crying in the next ward, a fellow came in with blood on his chin and his chest, holding his belly as if he was afraid that his guts would drop out, and a woman came in on a stretcher, screaming and rolling, and the assistants had to hold down her shoulders to keep her steady. One of the persons standing waiting said that the woman had taken poison, and immediately she and another woman began debating the merits and demerits of suicide; before that conversation ceased, the nurse came and told him that Stephanie had given birth to a girl.

He wanted to see her, but the nurse said that he could do so the following day.

When they were walking home, Lester said, 'Well, you must be relieved now.'

'Yes. But the police should do something about these hooligans. Is no joke to have them swooping down on innocent people like that. The police should do something about it.'

'It's not as simple as that,' Lester said. 'Much more is involved than action by the police.'

'Stephanie could have died, or the baby. We have too many hooligans in this city. Too many idle, ignorant people.'

'That is true,' Lester said.

'The police should do something about them, or the government if it comes to that. Something must be done.'

'Something must be done,' Lester said. 'But what?'

'I don't know. But that is why we have a police force, that is why we have a government, to protect the people. Look, tonight they even cut off a boy's hand, his mother crying and throwing down herself in the road. The police should be harder with them.'

'You can't blame the police. Already they're overworked,' Lester said. 'And I'm not sure that you could attach all the blame to the so-called hooligans, either.'

'Who'll you blame, then?'

'All of us have some share in the blame,' Lester said.

'Well, that's a fine one. That's a damn fine one. A setta young hooligans come down with guns and knives and iron bolts, wounding and chopping people, and you say all of us have blame in that. That's a fine one!'

'You see, Walter,' Lester said. 'We have to help them because we can't punish them. There's no way to punish them.'

'What you mean, we can't punish them?'

'It's like this: punishment is punishment, is effective only when the person punished is conscious that he has done wrong,' Lester said.

'You telling me that they don't know it's against the law to walk with knives and guns and iron bolts and shoot and wound people? That's what you saying?'

'Against what law?' Lester asked.

'The law,' Walter said. 'The law of the land.'

'But that's just what I'm telling you. They don't accept the law. They have their own laws, and the laws of the society are not necessarily their laws.'

'I don't see why the laws are not their laws. The law is for everybody,' Walter said.

'I'll tell you why they don't accept our laws. They don't accept the laws of society because, in the first place, society doesn't accept them. It appears to them that society wants to crush them. How can they accept society? And if they don't accept society, how can they accept the laws of society? This is quite simple, but many people don't consider this side of the problem.'

'They have to accept society. If you have to cat them and throw them in jail, they have to realize that the law is the law,' Walter said.

'No, Walter. You have to teach them; you can't force them.'

'You making joke, yes, Lester. I say teach them in jail, teach them with the cat whistling on their backside.'

'You're saying so because of what happened to Stephanie. If you look at the thing squarely, you wouldn't talk like that.'

'But I don't know how you'll teach them. If they don't learn in jail is because they don't want to learn.'

'Jail only makes them harder,' Lester said.

'What way they'll learn, Lester? What way?'

'I say, give them a purpose in life, give them a worthy goal, and give them a fifty-fifty chance to achieve it; try to understand and encourage them. That's the only way,' Lester said.

'What goal can we give them? What goal is there to give them?'

'That,' Lester said, 'is the problem. There seems to be nothing of lasting value that is at the same time sufficiently tangible. As a matter of fact, the goals of the supposed well-adjusted persons are nothing to shout about… And that's the truth.'

And that time he was silent and thoughtful, for there was much in what Lester had said.

Lester was right, the youngsters had no valuable goal. What goal can you give a young criminal, a young delinquent who has nothing, who has the whole big world against him, squeezing him, pushing him, telling him to move on; with the whole police force geared to fight him, with the whole lot of citizens watching for him to make a false move? What laws can you ask him to accept when you hold no law dear? When you accept laws only because it is convenient to you, when you flout those not in your direct interest, you, leading citizens of the nation? Lester was right. What was to be done? What could be done? What could he do? It was a hell of a situation.

Now he remembers how happy he was to see Stephanie feeling well and to see his little daughter, so tiny and full of life, and after Stephanie came from the hospital, he would hurry home from work just to look at his little baby.

And he remembers how good Mrs Walls was to them, how she helped Stephanie with the washing and the ironing while she was not well enough to take care of them herself. And he remembers the letter Stephanie received from Annabelle. It said that Annabelle was in England and it asked about Tom and about him, and for a bottle of home-made pepper sauce and a bottle of rum.

And he remembers that time when, nearing election time, Mr Sears and he went to the square to listen to the politicians, and how he stood there with his eyes looking up at the rostrum and heard the politicians tell about the schemes they had afoot for the development of the land, asking that they be returned to the legislature. And he remembers how, that same night, going home, he saw the beggars crouched in their rags on the cold pavements and passed the whores jammed at gateways, looking hawk-eyed for customers, and near the market, an old, old woman selling oranges, sleeping on herself, and above her head, stuck on the wall, a poster with the smiling face of an election candidate, marked, 'Vote Riley for progress'. Yes, and when he showed it to Mr Sears, Mr Sears said that Rome wasn't built in a day.

And he remembers too that time, right after the baby was christened, how his little brother Chris came to town to look for employment, and remained at his home for some time, and when he didn't get a job, disappeared, went back home. Back home, back home…

So many things a man remembers, so many things, like a

professor. He could write a book on memories alone. He could write about the things he had seen and heard and not take one thing from his imagination.